Night *of the* Dragon's Blood

NIGHT *of the* DRAGON'S BLOOD

William Pridgen

HODGE & BRADDOCK, *Publishers*

NIGHT OF THE DRAGON'S BLOOD

Copyright © 1997 by William Pridgen

All rights reserved. No part of this book may be reproduced in any form or by any electronic or mechanical means including information storage and retrieval systems without permission in writing from the publisher, except in the case of brief quotations embodied in critical articles and reviews. Inquiries should be addressed to Hodge & Braddock, Publishers, P. O. Box 1894, Palatka, Florida 32178.

Lyrics to the song "Counting the Ways" Copyright 1997 by Chordata Music. Used with permission.

Library of Congress Catalog Card Number: 96-78145

ISBN 0-9636512-6-9

First Edition

for
Doug and Jackie

Prologue

COUNTESS BORCA was livid. It was bad enough that Nazi Germany had invaded her country. But tonight the Nazis were inside her castle, their jackboots defiling its storied stone floors. In the spacious, medievally furnished main hall, several armed SS blackshirts stood about, keeping an eye on the pale, dark-haired, attractive Transylvanian lady, as she impatiently paced, slim and well-bosomed, in her red satin gown. To the Nazis' admiring eyes she looked about forty. They had to wonder how old, how ancient, she actually was, in that autumn of 1944, if the rumor was true about why they were ordered to secure Castle Borca.

Outside in the moonlit courtyard, a dark four-door sedan pulled up, a blackshirt behind the wheel. From the car's right rear door a pudgy SS officer emerged, his peaked cap knocked from his head by the door sill. Moments later the Countess stopped pacing and watched as the officer swaggered into the hall. He was an Obergruppenführer, the equivalent of general in the Schutzstaffel ranks. A Schütze (SS private) held the massive front door for him, the other men coming smartly to attention.

The Countess glowered as the officer walked over, a smug smile on his round porcine face. "Countess Borca," he said, politely removing his cap, which he checked nonchalantly for damage. "I am Obergruppenführer Dorsch of the Schutzstaffel." The Countess was in no mood for niceties. "Do you speak German?"

"Yes," she said coldly. "May I ask why the SS has invaded my castle?"

"To protect you, dear lady. You must come to no harm." He gestured toward a nearby oak table. "Shall we sit down?"

She went along grudgingly. "I've searched all Transylvania for someone like you," said Dorsch, as they sat down across from each other. He produced a silver cigarette case from a pocket. "I had almost decided that you didn't exist."

Opening the case, he held it toward her. "Care for a Lucky Reich?" he asked.

"No, thank you." She did not even look at the case.

"You do not smoke, Countess Borca?"

"No."

Leaning forward, Dorsch drew her attention to a mirror that was inside the case, and smiled. "No reflection on you," he said meaningfully.

Taken in, the Countess reacted violently, slapping the case out of the Nazi's hand, cigarettes flying in the air. They both rose to their feet in a huff. Then the Countess quickly regained her composure.

"I am sorry," she said calmly. "I do not like mirrors."

Dorsch smiled again, dismissing her effrontery. "Of course not. You are a vampire."

She strolled toward a large, leafy potted plant, which bore roselike red flowers. "Who told you such nonsense?" she asked.

"The local peasants." Dorsch followed her, two Schützes busily gathering up his smokes. "But I had to be sure. You know how superstitious they are."

Standing with her by the plant, Dorsch watched her smell one of the flowers. "A lovely plant," he said. "What is it called?"

"Dracaena," she said impatiently, her eyes still on the flower. "What do you want of me?"

"You must come with me, to Berlin."

PROLOGUE

She turned to look incredulously at Dorsch. "To Berlin? But why?"

"Because those are my orders."

She stared at him. He was smirking, but the smirk faded at the knowing look in her dark, haunting eyes. They both knew that the Third Reich's days were numbered—the end surely too near for Adolf Hitler's comfort—and the Countess could guess why this SS *Schweinehund* had been sent to find her.

"I will not go," she said with a defiantly raised chin.

"You will go," said the double-chinned Dorsch.

She turned and headed for the stairway, but stopped as two Schützes moved to block her way. She turned to glare back at the self-satisfied Dorsch.

"Do not try the bat thing," he warned. "You cannot escape us."

She tried the bat thing anyway. To the wonder of all in the room, the Countess transformed, seemingly sucked out of sight in an instant, replaced immediately by a big black bat. As the creature winged toward the top of the stairway, two SS men stationed there instinctively raised their weapons.

"Do not shoot!" yelled Dorsch. He knew vampires were reputedly immortal, yet he could just see himself handing a dead, lead-filled bat to the Führer.

The bat had already veered away. She was headed toward an open window across the wide hall, but before the bat could reach it, SS men banged the shutters to.

Dorsch and his men then watched the chiropteran fly in wide aimless circles overhead. "It is useless, my Countess!" Dorsch called to her with amusement. "You might as well come to roost!"

The bat responded with a pass that was far from aimless. Perhaps she could not escape, but she could at least give her captor something to remember.

Several SS men quickly came forward, pulling out handkerchiefs, almost falling over each other, to help clean the batshit from the Obergruppenführer's face.

Part One
Evita

1
Buenos Aires

HI HICKENLOOPER gazed at her face. He longed to cup it in his hands and kiss it, and to tell her how much he loved her. But the glass cover on the coffin prevented him from even touching her corpse. And besides, Hi only had a moment to look, for though he and Eva once had something special, he was now but one of the hundreds of thousands of mourners who would file past her coffin that week, some lovingly kissing the glass, others wiping it with handkerchiefs, removing the slobber and tears, before kissing it too. Hi, his light brown hair wet, his overcoat glistening, from waiting three hours in the rain, simply looked at her, achingly, for his allotted few seconds.

As he left the Ministry of Labor building where Eva Perón lay in state, Hi had no idea that he was being followed. Walking through the damp heart of Buenos Aires, Argentina, that evening, the handsome, thirty-three-year-old North American knew only that he was heartsick and cold. It was not Hi's first winter in the southern hemisphere, yet bone-chilling weather in August still struck him as weird. But then a lot of things were going to strike Hi as weird in that winter of '52.

Hi headed east on Avenida Corrientes, as did the dark-featured man in a pinstriped suit who was tailing him. Under his overcoat Hi wore a three-piece suit from El Sastre, the finest men's shop in Lima, Peru. He had bought the suit just for the funeral—if there was ever going to be one. It had been a week since Eva's death, and though Argentines were observing a thirty-day period of mourning, and though lines still formed for blocks, till late every evening, to see Eva's corpse, Buenos Aires's businesses had begun to reopen. Among them was Cuco's, one of numerous cabarets on Corrientes, where ten years earlier Hi and Eva first met.

She was María Eva Duarte back then, twenty-three, a poor girl from the town of Junín, in the big city trying to make it as an actress. Hi, also twenty-three, headquartered in Lima, had flown down to Buenos Aires after the first of his Amazonian expeditions. He needed some fun, and Buenos Aires, he had heard, was the Paris of Latin America. "When you get there," said an Argentine diplomat whom Hi met at a party in Lima, "go to Cuco's and meet my friend Cuco Rivera." With a smile the Argentine added, "Tell him Hermenegildo sent you, and Cuco will line you up good."

That sounded all right to Hi. On his first night in Buenos Aires in that spring of '42, he took a taxi from his hotel to Cuco's. It was a run-of-the-mill cabaret, most of its patrons well-dressed *porteños* ("port dwellers," as citizens of BA call themselves), quietly conversing while a young lady in a black silk dress sang in a way that seemed somehow confusing to the piano player who was accompanying her.

Hi looked sharp in his Brooks Brothers suit as he sat down at a table for two. Ordering a scotch, he asked the dour, middle-aged waiter if Cuco was around. The waiter said no, that "the rascal" would be around later. Hi assumed that the appellation was good-natured. It wasn't. Hi asked him to tell Cuco, if he got there soon, that "a friend of Herman and Gildo" wanted to meet him.

"A friend of who?" asked the waiter.

"Oh, just tell him a friend of some friends." Hi wasn't even sure if it was Herman or Gildo he had met at that party in Lima.

The waiter shrugged and left. Hi turned his attention to the pretty brunette who was singing. She didn't sing well at all. But watching her, Hi was reminded of a college course in aesthetics that he took as a sophomore. The professor, a man who was ugly as sin, posed the question, "What is beauty?" This lady wasn't gorgeous, some might say she was average, but Hi couldn't take his eyes off of her. Beauty, Hi realized that night, is that off of which you can't take your eyes. He wanted to know more about her. And he wished he could rewrite his term paper.

When the waiter returned with his drink, Hi asked him the lady's name. "Eva something," the waiter told him indifferently. "She doesn't really work here."

"Oh. This is amateur night?"

"No, I mean she is only working this evening."

Eva Duarte in fact was a desperate, unemployed actress doing yet another odd job: standing in for an acquaintance, the club's regular singer, who was sick with a cold caught from Cuco. Eva had come earlier that day from her dingy *pensión*, where the rent was past due, and begged Cuco to let her sing a few songs that night, for whatever he was willing to pay. Cuco, forty-five, a tall thin philanderer with most of his charm in his wallet, didn't need much convincing. He could easily have found a real singer, but he wanted to see more of Eva. She didn't want to see more of him, but didn't let him know it. In her struggle to eke out an existence without losing her integrity, Eva was learning to handle guys like Cuco who wanted favors in return for employment.

As Hi sat alone and listened to her sing, the other

patrons conversing, Eva appreciated his undivided attention. And she found Hi very attractive. As she sang, her eyes frequently met his. Before she was through, it was as if she were singing only to him. She even sang him a song in rote English.

Ten years later, walking once again into Cuco's, Hi found that the dimly lit cabaret looked almost the same (it had become a bit seedy), with assorted patrons having their little conversations—all centering, it seemed, on "Perón." But Hi didn't come there to find conversation. Nor to ask about Cuco, whom he fortunately never did meet. (Cuco was dead anyway, bludgeoned to death in 1948 by a cuckolded *pasaperro*, or professional dog walker.) Hi sat down at the bar next to no one and ordered a scotch on the rocks.

As he drank, Hi thought back to the moment when Eva Duarte came and sat down at his table, after finishing her songs and going backstage. Hi had sent her a note via the waiter, inviting her to join him for a drink. It didn't take her long to respond.

Hi tried now to remember where he and Eva sat. As Hi turned to look over the room, Hernán Soto, sipping alone at a table, felt a momentary twinge of fear. It was Soto, a swarthy, compact, thirty-eight-year-old fellow with a black moustache, who had tailed Hi from the ministry building. He now wondered if Hi, whose eyes fleetingly fell upon him, might somehow recognize him. But then Soto knew that that was impossible.

No, Hi couldn't pinpoint the table or spot. But as he turned back to his drink and his thoughts of Evita, he remembered the Spanish conversation as if he had tape-recorded it.

"I'm Eva."
"I'm Hi."

"Hi, Hi."
"Hi."
"What do you do, Hi?"
"I look for lost cities."
"Sounds neat."
"It's no picnic."
"Nothing is. As you say in English, 'It's a jungle out there.'"
"That's pretty good. How much English do you know?"
"I know lots of slang words."
"Know any real dirty ones?"
"Sure. Want to hear one?"

They would talk dirty later. For the moment, Eva briefly described her life—the impoverished childhood, the dream of becoming a film star, the reality of occasional bit parts in stage and radio plays, her one-night charade as a singer—but the whole thing depressed her, so she preferred to hear about Hi. He told her how he had majored in business administration at the University of Florida, class of '41, in preparation for one day heading Hickenlooper Foods, the large Florida corporation that his father Edgar and late German-born mother Erika had built from a burger stand in Apalachicola. As for the war, Hi was 4F, though he was quick to tell Eva that his clubfoot was "hardly noticeable." Indeed people unaware of the foot simply noticed—if it registered at all—a slight spring in Hi's gait. Aside from that deformity, Hi was a fine physical specimen, and would have served proudly had Uncle Sam wanted him. His fluent German—learned mostly from his garrulous immigrant mother, his father being first generation and indifferent to Deutsch—might have come in handy in military intelligence work. Hi would have pushed for it, but Edgar, though a patriot, had plans for his son that could not be delayed for some military desk job. Hi acquiesced, and his language proficiency, as far as he knew, was never discussed at the draft board.

Edgar's plans for his son did not include the corporate life either. Not yet. That still lay far in Hi's future, which was just fine with Hi. The young college graduate had an enviable mission, ordained by his father, before becoming a CEO. For Edgar, as a result of having participated, as a teenage hired hand, in the discovery in 1911 of the ruins of Peru's Macchu Picchu, had an abiding if quixotic desire to make an archeological name for himself. Now a wealthy man, Edgar had the financial resources to mount the necessary South American expeditions, if only his son Hi—who at UF had dutifully taken courses in archeology and Spanish—could actually go find some ruins.

Needing a break after his first long, futile foray into the Amazon rain forest, Hi had come down to see Buenos Aires, and fate—or "Herman and Gildo"—had brought him to Cuco's and Eva. Hi and Eva had a two-year affair. Hi was wildly in love. He wanted to marry her. He wanted to give her all she could ever want, or at least try to. And Eva loved Hi. But she met someone else, and had to make a difficult choice. She left Hi for a politicking Argentine colonel. Hi was crushed. She was the first thing he ever really wanted that he couldn't have. There was no getting over her. For the next eight years, as Eva rose to be Argentina's first lady, she had haunted Hi's mind. Now she was dead, and would haunt him forever.

Soto, sipping his drink, wondered why the young, good-looking, well-heeled fellow he was tailing seemed so despondent. It made it easier, though, should Soto get the order, to put Hi Hickenlooper out of his misery.

2
Southwest of Manaus

DEEP IN THE AMAZON rain forest, as nightfall approached, Julian Bates and John Crowley stopped to make camp. The dimming sky showed through gaps in the dense jungle canopy above them. The two sturdy Americans, both in their early thirties, had been exploring for days without luck, accompanied by two Peruvian and four Brazilian assistants. At the moment they were some three hundred miles southwest of Manaus, Brazil. The nearest village was some five miles to the east, on a branch of the Purús River.

Bates sent one of the Peruvians to check out a thick line of vegetation several yards to the west. In the heart of the rain forest, such heavy undergrowth was not typically found. Its presence was sign of a nearby clearing or some other break in the canopy, which ordinarily blocked out too much light for dense plant life to develop below. But Bates, tired and frustrated, didn't expect the Peruvian to find anything of significance.

"Another day shot to hell," Bates complained, wiping sweat from his face with a sleeve.

"Don't worry," Crowley told his partner. "There's a lost city somewhere."

"Hi Hickenlooper's somewhere too," Bates shot back. "I'm worried about him beating us to it."

"I told you, he's in Argentina. Quit worrying."

" 'Quit worrying,' hell. He'll be back."

The mild-mannered Crowley had to laugh. "Hi Hickenlooper," he pointed out, "has never found anything."

"That makes it worse," Bates griped. "He's overdue. He's been around. He knows where not to look. And you know what bugs me the most? He's rich. He doesn't *have* to find anything."

They both drank some water from their canteens. "Lot of bats coming out," Crowley noted, watching bats flit about overhead. Bates looked up at the little flying mammals. Their seemingly coordinated behavior puzzled both men. And *these* bats didn't seem all that little.

"Jefes! Vengan!" yelled the Peruvian who had been sent to scout the thick line of undergrowth to the west. He had just come back out of the thicket, and from the excitement in his voice it was clear he had found something extraordinary. Bates, Crowley, and the rest of the team followed him back through the dense undergrowth to see his discovery.

"Miren!" said the wide-eyed Peruvian, as they emerged from the wall of vegetation. In an extensive clearing before them the explorers saw four large, thatch-roofed wooden buildings, well spaced with cleared ground between them. They saw no one about in the gathering darkness.

Bates was not impressed. This was no lost city. "Big deal," he said bitterly.

"Whose place do you reckon this is?" asked the fascinated Crowley.

"Who cares?" Bates muttered.

Crowley was particularly intrigued by the far building facing them, a two-story structure with a balcony, from the railing of which hung a large scarlet banner. On the banner was a swastika, emblazoned in black.

"Nazis?" Crowley said wonderingly. "What the hell are

they doing out here?"

"What's that word there over the balcony?" Bates asked. He had grudgingly taken interest in that building too.

"Looks like German," Crowley said. The word was impressively embossed on a plaque in Gothic script. Crowley tried to read it aloud, though ignorant of its meaning: "Neu... an... fang?"

Neither Bates nor Crowley, nor any of their assistants, as they were staring at this mysterious jungle compound, noticed that several of those odd-acting, somewhat oversized bats, virtually invisible against the darkening sky, had begun hovering over them. Finally the men heard the flutter of wings, as the bats descended to the ground right before them. By the time the creatures touched ground, they were not even bats anymore. Bates, Crowley, and the others found themselves confronted instead by a frightening group of pale but strapping men wearing jackboots, black shirts and breeches. They looked like something straight out of Nazi Germany, if not out of hell itself.

Crowley was the first who managed to say anything, his throat constricted by terror at the dumbfounding advent of these menacing beings. And he tried his damndest to make it sound nice.

"Hi, fellas. What can we do for ya?"

3

Looking for Hi

McKAY KNOCKED on the front door and waited, looking over the pleasant surroundings. The colonial mansion was in Miraflores, the ritziest suburb of Lima. The fifty-year-old, thin-haired Britisher, looking trim and fit in his dark conservative suit, had been scouring the Peruvian capital city all day; he hoped his search was nearly over as the ornate door opened and a *mestizo* butler appeared.

"Sí?" asked the butler, looking McKay over.

"My name is McKay. I want to speak with Diego Vara."

The butler responded in heavily accented English: "And why should Diego Vara want to speak with you?"

McKay stared at him soberly, though amused at the folly of the butler's query. McKay was only there, after all, to help save the free world. "I'm looking for Hi Hickenlooper," McKay said evenly. "Mister Vara should know where he is."

Diego at that moment was upstairs, jitterbugging with a young Latin beauty in a sitting room. The 78-rpm record playing on the hi-fi was the throbbing "Sweet Workin' Woman," the biggest hit of 1952 among North American blacks. Diego would slip it out, on such occasions as this, like a secret weapon—as if Lima's most eligible native son needed one. Diego was thirty-one, handsome with raven-black hair, and financially set for life through the Vara family inheritance. But in romance every little bit helps, and nothing, thought Diego as he watched the Latina's shapely, swinging hips, turns women on like "Sweet Workin' Woman."

"Oh, Diego, I love this!" the girl squealed, having never heard anything like it, as she followed Diego's effortless lead. "Where did you get that recording?"

"Hi smuggled it in from the states."

"What do the gringos call it?"

"Rhythm and blues."

"Rrrrrrhythm and blues!" she trilled with delight as they danced. "What will they think of next?"

The butler appeared at the door. "A McKay here to see you!" he yelled above the music.

"McKay?" asked Diego, continuing to dance. The name rang no bell. "What does he want?"

"To find Hi Hickenlooper."

The Latina suddenly stopped dancing, a look of alarm on her face. "He is from the police," she said impulsively. "They've found out."

"Found out what?" asked Diego.

"That Hi has been smuggling in blues!"

Diego smiled, told her not to worry, and suggested she play the raunchy flip side until he got back. Diego went downstairs to the library, where his waiting British visitor stood examining Diego's collection of pre-Columbian pornographic pottery.

"Mr. McKay?" asked Diego, walking in.

"Yes," McKay said, quickly setting down the piece of twelfth-century smut he was holding. He self-consciously wiped his hand on his coat before shaking Diego's hand. "Thank you for seeing me."

"Care for a drink?" Diego walked over to a well-stocked portable bar.

"Something with pisco. Good stuff."

Diego smiled. "Just getting to know Peru, eh?" He began fixing their drinks. "And what can I do for you?"

"I've been looking for Hi. High and low."

"Who is Lowe?"

"I've been looking for *Hi* high and low." McKay waited, Diego handing him his pisco cocktail. "Do you know where he is?"

"Why do you wish to see Hi?"

"I've got a job for him."

Diego chuckled as he walked over to a chair. "You don't know much about Hi," he opined, sitting down.

"What do you mean?"

"Hi is the sole heir of Hickenlooper Foods. He is hardly in need of a job."

"It's not a question of money," McKay said. "Or of food. And you are wrong. I know all there is to know about Hi Hickenlooper." McKay strolled about, sipping his drink, occasionally handling some pottery, as he continued. "He is a man who must labor for his father's obsession. His father was with Hiram Bingham, in 1911, when Bingham discovered Macchu Picchu, Lost City of the Incas. And ever since Hi grew up, his father, sparing no expense, has sent him time and again into the Amazon jungle, in search of El Dorado, or whatever lost city he can find."

Diego was listening with an impassive expression. McKay was indeed well-informed about Diego's North American friend. Hi had taken Diego along on his last trip home, to the Florida panhandle town of Apalachicola, less than two months before. And the conversation Diego witnessed, on a patio of the Hickenlooper estate, between the formerly carefree, outgoing Hi and his imposing, sixty-two-year-old father, was searingly fresh in Diego's memory. It was then that Diego had first learned the true depth of Hi's current despair. The conversation now came back to Diego as McKay rattled on.

"Going hard on the liquor, aren't you?" Edgar Hickenlooper asked disapprovingly, as the family butler served Hi a second drink. Diego was still nursing his first. They were sitting on a patio on a hot day in June.

"It's been a long trip," Hi said absently. "Need a little refreshment."

"There's Royal Crown in the fridge. It used to be your favorite."

"I gave 'em up, Dad. In South America an RC's just too hard to find." Diego, as he listened uncomfortably, could vouch well for that. It was Hi who had introduced him to RCs and moon pies. Pepsi Colas were hard to find too.

"How are things at Hickenlooper Foods?" Hi asked, though he wasn't really interested.

"Let's cut the small talk," said his father. "I wasn't pleased with your last expedition report."

"Why not?"

"You didn't find anything."

"I'm still looking."

"Nearly one million dollars, Hi. One million. That's how much I have squandered so far on your fruitless expeditions."

"We're not looking for fruit. Give me a break, Dad. I didn't ask for this, you know. You sent me down there."

"To find something! Is that asking too much? Have I overburdened you with responsibility?"

"Perhaps I should go," said Diego, starting to rise.

"Stay put," Hi said. "You're like family."

Ignoring Diego, Edgar stared hard at Hi. "I could have made you stay here and learn the food business, but I didn't. You've got a whole jungle to play in down there."

"I hadn't thought of it that way," Hi said wryly. "I owe you a lot."

Diego again started to rise. "I'll just—"

"Stay put," Hi repeated.

"I promised Hiram Bingham," Edgar said with frustration, "after we found Macchu Picchu, that my newborn son—the son to whom I gave the name Hiram—would carry on, that even greater discoveries lay ahead."

"I've let you down, Dad, you and ol' Hiram." It was a bitterly mock apology. "I'm still looking."

"And drinking yourself to an early grave. You're becoming a sot, and all because of that Argentine woman."

That struck a raw nerve. Diego would never forget Hi's pained look. Edgar didn't let up. "I know all about it. She left you for Juan Perón. And now rumor has it she's dying of cancer."

"You got it right, Dad." Hi's voice was thick with emotion. Diego knew that Hi had become troubled, depressed. But not till hearing that conversation between Hi and Edgar did Diego appreciate how much. Hi had lost his mother to cancer two years before. Now it has to be tough, Diego thought that day on the patio, to be crazy about a terminally ill woman who dumped you.

"Forget her, Hi," Edgar lectured. "You can't grieve forever. If she's dying, you couldn't have had her long anyway."

"Gee, Dad, you're right," Hi said sardonically. "Every cloud has a silver lining."

"Take your break, then get back to that jungle. Find me a city, any lost city, before someone else beats you to it."

Diego, remembering, sadly shook his head. He began listening once more to McKay: "Hi's Peruvian mentor in archeology and exploration was your father, the late Francisco Vara." McKay glanced around at the luxury of Diego's digs, and added, "And you, when you have the spare time, have accompanied Hi on a number of his fruitless expeditions."

"We're not looking for fruit," Diego found himself saying.

"You must know where Hi is. I've been all over Lima."

"He's in mourning," Diego half-whispered. "He has lost her again."

"Lost who?"

"His Evita."

"Evita—?"

"Perón." Diego noted McKay's stunned look. "She left Hi for Perón. High and dry."

"Who is Drye?"

"She left *Hi* high and dry."

McKay paused to think. Hi's involvement with Eva Perón was an unexpected complication. And possibly disastrous for the cause. But McKay would have to deal with that later. "No doubt he's in mourning," McKay allowed, "but where is Hi physically?"

"This job you're to offer. What is it?"

"I will discuss that with him," McKay said.

It was a tactless response. Diego finished his drink and got up. "Then you will have to find him," he said politely. "Good luck. Can I help you with anything else?"

McKay watched Diego set down his glass. McKay had to say something quick or this visit was over. "What if I told you the job involves Adolf Hitler?"

Diego stared at him. "*The* Adolf Hitler?"

"The one and only."

"Are you saying he's alive?"

McKay finished his drink. "No," he said cryptically, "I wouldn't say that." He handed the glass to his host.

Diego, setting down the glass, wondered who this man represented. "Who do you work for?" Diego asked.

"I can't tell you that."

Diego stared at him for a moment, then shrugged. Diego turned as if to leave.

"On second thought," McKay relented, "why not? An international intelligence organization called IQ."

Diego turned again to McKay. "IQ?"

"The Intelligence Quorum."

Diego had never heard of it. "Must be new."

"On the contrary. It was originally founded by Attila the Hun. Only now we're the good guys." IQ had evolved, from its humble beginnings as a network of spies scouting villages for Attila to pillage, into an international agency working, in McKay's words, "for the good of mankind." As the Britisher explained to Diego, IQ worked much like an Interpol covert-operations division. The supersecret agency worked against all forms of tyranny, helping root out the kind of political criminals who caused so many world problems. And free nations voted before action was taken. A quorum was required, hence the agency's modern-day name.

"Can you tell me where Hi is?" McKay asked again.

Diego considered, as he studied his visitor. If this really involved Hitler, he had no choice but to help. Diego wasn't sure he agreed with IQ as an overall concept. Too much meddling in other people's affairs. But Hitler? Definitely worth rooting out. "I will take you to Hi."

"Do we have far to go?" asked the grateful McKay.

"About two thousand miles. Buenos Aires."

4

Umwandlungpfuhl

TERRIFIED BATES stared down at the water. Hands bound, he had been led by two SS Schützes to the very edge of the platform, where they then bound his ankles. Now the slightest loss of balance could mean death by drowning in the pool, which was lit underwater, a few feet below him. In his fear, and concentrating on his balance, Bates was not even aware of his audience. There in the compound's Gebäude Vier (Building Four), on a bank of seats, in the darkness beyond the pool, sat several SS men, in their black shirts and jackboots, silently watching and waiting. The only sound, faintly heard, was that of a gasoline-powered generator, one of several used on the compound for electrical energy.

To Bates's side on the platform stepped Obergruppenführer Kegel. He was a pale, lean fellow with the meanest smile that Bates had ever seen. Kegel looked back at a Schütze watching from the window of the Water Control Room (Wasserkontrollzimmer), only ten feet away at the rear of the platform. In the Water Control Room, most of the meters and other gadgetry were unimportant, being only for show. (The intended impression was of being in a German U-2 boat, though minus the periscope.) One of the gadgets that *was* important was a large lever near the window, where the Schütze stood waiting. This gadget was the Grosser Wichtiger Hebel, or Large Important Lever. At Kegel's signal, the Schütze stepped over and pulled the thing down.

Bates and Kegel then watched as an underwater tunnel from an adjoining water tank opened in the side of the pool, and a large school of piranhas—small ravenous fish with razor-sharp teeth—began streaming into the pool.

Kegel's smile broadened as Bates's eyes widened. "Piranhas," said Kegel admiringly. "Such fascinating little creatures. They can devour a man in seconds, leaving nothing but blood and bones. How is my English?" Kegel was brushing up on English in his spare time, which he had plenty of.

"What?" said the distracted Bates. "Oh. Real good." Bates suddenly saw a slim chance to live. "But it could be much better. Can I be your tutor?"

Kegel smiled. "We call this our conversion pool. *Unserer Umwandlungpfuhl—*"

"I'm converted!" Bates assured him. "Really I am. I believe in the Reich and all that."

Kegel looked at Bates with disdain. "I don't mean converting the mind, you fool," Kegel sneered. "We convert your body, into blood. What do you think we live on out here?"

Though Kegel didn't mention it to Bates, piranhas were even lethal to vampires. That startling discovery had been made when the late Schütze Vogel, while binding a captive on the platform, accidentally fell into the pool. The piranhas made short work of him. As far as anyone knew, Schütze Vogel had never come back.

As Bates watched the piranhas swim around, Kegel enjoyed going into detail on conversion. It was a good chance to practice his English with a native speaker. "First the piranhas do their work. Then we drain the pool, separating, through a special osmotic process, the impure fluid—"

"Impure fluid?" Bates interrupted, not taking his eyes off the fish.

"The water. Leaving nothing but blood."

"Why so much trouble? Why not just draw out some blood when you need it? I got plenty!"

"Oh, we do," Kegel smiled. "With some people. But others—special ones—go into our pool."

"Why be choosy?" The captive was trying to be as helpful as possible. "Why not just extract? It's easier."

"Easier, yes. But no fun!"

Chuckling at his own humor, Kegel slapped the bound man chummily on the back. Screaming, Bates toppled into the water.

The piranhas wasted no time. As the feeding frenzy commenced, the SS men leaned forward in their seats, to watch Bates being converted into blood and bones. The SS men watched rather impassively, as this act was becoming old hat. Still, for these guys—most of them in the jungle going on seven years—almost anything passed for entertainment.

What, they kept wondering over the nightly blood rations in their Gebäude Zwei drink hall—*what* was the Führer waiting for?

5

The Woman in Black

HI COULDN'T HELP IT. For the second night in a row he was sitting at the bar in Cuco's. And for the second night in a row, Soto was having to watch him. Hi was on his fourth scotch, and each drink, far from drowning anything, seemed only to intensify his memories of Evita. At the moment he was remembering all too well the conversation in 1944 in which the woman he would always love told him it was over. They had met only two years before, and for the first year or so what a time it had been, full of passion and play. But things began changing between Hi's second and third unsuccessful Amazonian expeditions. By '44 Eva was a well-known radio actress. She had dyed her hair blonde. And she had met Colonel Juan Perón.

Hi and Eva were having coffee, soon after Hi's return to Buenos Aires from his third expedition, in a *confitería*—one of the city's innumerable sidewalk cafes—when she finally told him what was bothering her. It was devastating news.

"I can't believe what you're saying."
"He asked me. I said yes."
"You're going to marry Juan Perón?"
"Please understand, Hi. It's been wonderful, what you and I have had together. But I must think of the future. Juan is the Minister of War—"
"I thought he was the Secretary of Labor."

"*He is Minister of War in the morning and Secretary of Labor in the afternoon. With luck, or a coup, he could be the next president.*"
"*You're going to give up your career?*"
"*With Juan I'll be politically involved. There are things more important than radio soap operas.*"
"*I agree. So give your career up for me, not Perón.*"
"*If I married you, Hi—you with your lost cities, so far from Argentina—*"
"*Forget the lost cities. We'll go live in the states. We'll get politically involved.*"
"*But your father, he—*"
"*Forget about Dad. We'll go back to the old hometown. You'll love it in Apalachicola.*"
"*But don't you see, Hi? I don't want to go to—uh . . .*"
"*Apalachicola? Then you name it. New York? We'll go to Chicago.*"
"*I don't want to go to New York or Chicago.*"
"*Why not?*"
"*Because Chicago is . . .*"
"*Not your kind of town?*"
"*I am Argentine, Hi. This is my home, my people.*"
"*No problem. We'll stay here.*"
"*I'm sorry, Hi. My future is with Juan.*"

Hi bristled at the memory. *My future is with Juan.* How Hi hated the man, though he had never met him. Juan, with his political ambitions, had made Eva thirst for power. She had good intentions. She knew what it was like to be poor, and wanted to help Argentines who still were. But Hi wondered, as he signaled for a refill, if Eva might still be alive had she not married Perón. The colonel had been married once before, and that wife died of cancer too. Not that Juan Perón was some kind of carcinogen, but Hi still had to wonder.

Then suddenly something happened that *really* caused Hi to wonder. Glancing over his shoulder, he caught sight of what seemed almost an apparition. It was strange, to begin with, to see a woman in mourner's apparel in a cabaret. Of course all of Buenos Aires was in mourning, so this woman in black, with pale but youthful features behind a thin veil, would not be out of place outside Cuco's. But Hi was struck by something else as he gazed at her. And it wasn't just the way she stood there, looking the room over as if with nostalgia, or how Hi had somehow failed to notice her entrance in the large mirror behind the bar into which he'd been staring, however vacantly, all evening. What struck Hi, what had him staring transfixed at her, was who she seemed to be. She was a dead ringer, behind that thin veil, for Evita. She looked pale, though. What Hi could see of her hair looked brunette—just like young Eva Duarte's.

Her sad eyes, looking over the room, moved to Hi. They were Eva's eyes, and they clearly registered surprise at the sight of him.

"Eva?" he said, loud enough to draw a few curious looks, including one from Soto, who was also regarding the woman.

Under Hi's gaze she turned hurriedly to leave. Hi rose quickly to follow, but just before reaching the door he ran into a large clenched fist that seemed to come out of nowhere. It caught him squarely on the forehead, just above the bridge of his nose. Knocked out momentarily, Hi found himself groggily looking up from the floor at a large, muscular man in a business suit and hat. The man was pale-faced and grinning. With a courteous nod toward Hi, he quickly turned and went out.

Hi gingerly felt his nose, found no damage. Struggling to his feet, he again tried to rush out, but a strong hand on his arm jerked him back. Hi turned to look into the face of a tall, broad Latino. He was the cabaret's bouncer, and his smile said he enjoyed his job.

"You didn't pay for your drinks," the bouncer cheerfully told Hi.

Still seeing stars, Hi hastily took out a large bill and handed it to the bouncer. "A roundhouse," Hi said. "No! I mean a round for the house."

The bouncer thanked him, and Hi hurried out. Ever alert, the bouncer then grabbed Soto, who was rushing for the door after Hi.

"You didn't pay for yours either," the bouncer told Soto.

It was foggy outside, which, added to four scotches and a blow to the head, didn't help Hi's visibility. But the street was well lit, and Hi reached it just in time to spot the woman and his assailant turn the corner onto Calle Florida.

Hurrying to the corner and around it, Hi could barely make out through the fog what appeared to be the same couple, going into a shop down the street. Calle Florida was a street of chic shops and restaurants, for pedestrians only. Making his way through evening shoppers, Hi was unsure which store the couple had gone into. He began walking along looking in windows. At the third window he stopped. There in a clothing shop stood the couple Hi had seen enter, both with their backs to the window. Seeing the shapely, black-clothed lady from behind, Hi was sure that it was the woman who had fled Cuco's, and that the big guy in the suit who stood near her was the oaf who had slugged him.

Hurrying into the shop, Hi went straight to the woman, took hold of her arm, and turned her around. "Eva," he blurted, before he realized that this wasn't the woman.

The man with her grabbed Hi's arm and spun him around. Hi just had time to see that this wasn't the oaf. The man's fist slammed into Hi's face, knocking Hi backwards into toppling clothes racks. The blow had caught him squarely in the forehead, just above the bridge of his nose.

What a coincidence, Hi thought as he woke up minutes later.

After paying for the damage to the shop, Hi headed straight for the Ministry of Labor building, where *somebody* still lay in state. As usual, Hi didn't know he was being followed. The only thing on his mind, besides a terrific headache, was finding out who, or what, he had seen in the cabaret.

I've got to find a dead woman, Hi thought, so I might as well start with the corpse.

6
Roosevelt Redux

THERE WAS WAR in Kegel's quarters. Obergruppenführer Dorsch, a bit trimmer and certainly paler than during the European war years, was pitting his toy soldiers against Obergruppenführer Kegel's, and getting the worst of it. For cannons he and Kegel used little lead pipes with caps on one end, with holes in the caps to light firecracker fuses.

"We are supposed to be conquering the world," Dorsch said bitterly, repositioning some soldiers. "Instead, we rot in this jungle while the Führer keeps writing his memoirs. How many volumes? You must speak to him, Kegel."

"It would not do any good," Kegel said, carefully aiming a cannon.

"But this could go on forever. Did we become vampires for nothing? We are not getting any younger."

"True. We are also not getting any older." After lighting a firecracker fuse, Kegel plugged his ears with his fingers. "Did you know," he said, "he has spent two weeks trying to think up a title?" The firecracker went off in the cannon, blasting a marble into Dorsch's front ranks.

"What has he come up with?" Dorsch asked, doing a quick body count.

"He leans toward *Why the Thing in Europe Went Wrong*."

"Pah!" said Dorsch irreverently, aiming his cannon in turn. "He should be honest, no excuses. He should call it

How I Bombed in Berlin." Dorsch lit his firecracker.

"He shouldn't call it anything," Kegel said, again plugging his ears, "if it never gets finished."

The Nazi vampires at Neuanfang had reason to complain. The first compound had been built in '44, before the war ended, in anticipation of the German defeat. Its builders, a combination of Nazis and laborers contracted by Brazilian sympathizers, were not even aware of its purpose. After Hitler and his initial SS cadre—vampires all, thanks to the exploited Countess Borca—moved in, the Führer spent two years toiling away on his memoirs, leaving Dorsch, Kegel, and the others with little to do but maintain the blood supply. Then Hitler made a humiliating discovery. The lower section of the neighboring Aripuana River was known as Rio Roosevelt.

No way was the Führer going to be headquartered by a river named, even in part, after FDR. So a new compound had to be built, this one over toward the Purús, with whatever labor force and materials the SS could secure. It was almost a three-year project, with most of the building supplies brought in piecemeal by a war-surplus helicopter out of Manaus. The poor non-suspecting, non-SS laborers were doomed to be captives, part of the new blood supply. And after all that, with Hitler relocated and back at work on his memoirs, it was discovered that Rio Roosevelt had been named after Theodore, not Franklin. Hitler pretended that that didn't matter. "You've seen one Roosevelt," he blustered, "you've seen them all."

Now the vampires languished at Neuanfang (New Beginning)—or, as some of them privately referred to the relocated compound, Neu*neu*anfang. Supplies such as gasoline were picked up when needed through a lone nearby village, visited only by the Hauptsturmführer with one or two Schützes, whom the villagers simply thought to be "soldiers." Morale on the compound was critically low. Even Kegel and Dorsch, with their silly little war games, were about to lose all their marbles.

"I'll tell you something else," Dorsch said as he lit another firecracker. "The Führer worries too much about *her*."

"About who?" Kegel had his ears plugged again.

Dorsch's cannon fired, sending a marble right past Kegel's elbow and deep into the Paraná pine wall behind him.

"His woman," Dorsch said, self-conscious as Kegel looked back at the new hole in his wall. "She means nothing!" Dorsch vehemently added.

Dorsch soon surrendered to Kegel. Humiliating as always, but on the usual lenient terms: Dorsch was getting good at personally replacing pine panels in Kegel's walls.

7

Body Double

WHEN HI REACHED the ministry, people were queued as usual in the cold down both sides of the street, which was heavily lined with flowers. But Hi wasn't going to wait. Going into the building, he headed straight for the upper lobby, ignoring the two lines of people standing patiently on the stairway as he went striding up past them. Some looked at Hi curiously, others reacted verbally with anger, drawing the attention of a policeman in front of the stairway. But Hi, jerking his arm from a couple of people who grabbed it, didn't care. He had one thing on his mind, and he knew he would have only moments—assuming he even got to the coffin—before he would be apprehended.

In his favor was the element of surprise. Striding into the upper lobby, where all the complaints on the stairway had been unheard or were incomprehensible, Hi quickly stepped through one of the two lines, right up to the coffin. He had already decided what specifically to look for first, then he would try for a more general impression of the face, before they took him away.

As rushed as he was, Hi still marveled, as he gazed down through the glass, at how much like Eva it was. But then he saw—or rather didn't see—what he had decided to look for, and that for Hi was the clincher. As one policeman took hold of Hi's left arm, and another the right arm, Hi glanced anxiously at both officers and announced, almost jubilantly, "It's not her!"

The people standing in two lines outside watched with amazement as the two policeman came hauling Hi out of the building by his arms. What amazed them the most was how the man being hauled seemed almost to enjoy it. When the policemen got Hi out past the lines, they heaved him right into the street.

The fog hampered traffic in Buenos Aires that evening. Luigi Sandoni, a forty-year-old Italian immigrant driving past the ministry, was already exhausted from twelve hours of longshoring, when he saw a man land sprawling on his face right in front of his '38 Ford. Luigi slammed on his breaks, and brought his Ford to a screeching halt, within a foot or so of the man, who simply got up off the pavement with an odd little smile on his face.

Luigi then saw the culprits, two policemen chuckling smugly at the curb. Before Luigi could see anything else, a car in the fog behind him, tires squealing, slammed into the back of his Ford. Irate and with whiplash, Luigi got out. He looked at the considerable damage to his car, then yelled fiercely at the policemen: "Look what you did! Why don't you watch where you're throwing people?"

Hi was already walking away. He knew what he needed to know, and it had filled him with exhilaration. Eva was alive. He knew it. What's more, she had come nostalgically to Cuco's. Why? She had only worked there, ten years before, for *one night*. Hi was sure he knew why she was drawn there. It was where she and Hi had first met. Hi knew that Eva still loved him.

But he still had to find her. He had to know what she was up to, and why she had fled.

As usual Hi didn't know, as he left the scene of the accident, that he was still being followed.

8

Holes in His Story

LYING NUDE ON THE BED, in a cheap Buenos Aires hotel room, Jorge Ballesteros, with a mixture of excitement and wonder, watched in the dark—the only light was from a street lamp outside—as his pickup removed the last of her clothes. The soft-spoken, fifty-four-year-old banker, walking out of a theater, had spotted her, clothed in black, bareheaded, leaning invitingly by herself against the wall of a building, in the unusually thick evening fog. As he walked toward her, she glanced once toward him, but as he stepped to her side, she continually gazed off, so that he didn't see her full face. Strange, Jorge thought, but if it weren't for that brunette hair....

"I am Jorge," he said. "Who are you?"

She kept gazing off. "María," she said.

"How much would you cost me, María?"

After a moment, she said, "One thousand pesos." Her Spanish was accented, Jorge thought she was German. He didn't know that the accent was fake.

He was amazed by that profile. "It's a deal."

It was a short walk to the hotel. Now, in the darkened room, as she crawled onto the foot of the bed and began moving over his body, kissing it as she slowly advanced, he was struck more than ever by how much she looked like Eva Perón. He knew, of course, that Eva was dead, and that the idea of Eva as a streetwalker, dead or alive, was preposterous. Still, Jorge couldn't help thinking that the fear-tinged excitement he felt must be something like necrophilia.

When her mouth reached the side of his neck, Jorge felt her tongue lick the skin. Then he thought he felt something else. "It feels like you're biting my neck," Jorge said with a nervous chuckle. She continued without answering. "You're not actually biting, though, are you? You're just nibbling, right?" She still didn't answer, and he was too thrilled, or too scared, to move, so that he was unable to see her mouth, or the two streams of blood that were running down the side of the bed sheet.

Then she finished and propped up on her hands. To his horror, there was blood on her lips. She licked them, and a drop hit his chest.

"What have you done?" he was scarcely able to ask. She quickly rose from the bed to start dressing. "What are you?" he asked, afraid to put a hand to his neck.

As María hurriedly dressed, Jorge went from the bed to a mirror. He gasped at the sight of the two bloody punctures in the side of his neck. "My God," he said, rushing to pull a handkerchief out of his pants on the floor.

"I am sorry," María said, even sounding like Eva Perón, as Jorge had heard her in newsreels. There was no German accent, but she spoke very quietly, rushed. "There should be no effect. One quickie, as they say, doesn't do it."

"No effect?" Jorge was pressing the handkerchief to his wounds. "What about these two holes in my neck?"

"I am sorry," she repeated. "They will heal."

Jorge looked at them again in the mirror. When he turned again, she was gone. On a table he saw his one thousand pesos.

It would be late before Jorge went home. He always

dreaded going home anyway, but how could he possibly explain this one to Nita?

He knew his fifty-year-old, dour-looking wife would be standing there in her houserobe, glaring at him, waiting for an explanation about where he had been. Well, for once he would tell her the truth. More or less.

Still stunned by his experience, he walked into the house about midnight, the lapel of his overcoat turned up over the side of his neck. Nita had walked into the parlor to meet him. She stood there in her houserobe, glaring at him, waiting for an explanation about where he had been. "This had better be good," Nita said.

Jorge, with a glassy look in his eyes, plopped down in a chair, preparing himself to tell her the truth. "I was attacked by a vampire," he said, sounding like he didn't believe it himself. "She looked just like Eva Perón."

Nita stared at him. She was too amazed to be angry. He had more imagination than she had given him credit for. "Look," he said, and lowered the coat lapel, exposing his wounds to her.

Nita walked over to him. Leaning down, she took a good, close look at the two holes, ringed with dried blood, in his neck. Then she straightened up and looked at him disdainfully.

"Only you would do that," she said. "Only you would punch holes in your neck to back up such a story."

Nita turned to head back for bed. As she was leaving the room, she mockingly quoted him: "She looked just like Eva Perón."

9

Footsteps at Midnight

AFTER HIS NEAR-DEATH EXPERIENCE in front of the ministry, Hi had gone back to Cuco's. He hoped to get some clue about what was happening by asking witnesses what they knew about the oaf who had slugged him. All anyone knew was that the man looked powerful, Nordic, and had knocked the hell out of Hi. Yes, the man had come in with a woman in black. One fellow, half-drunk and still spooked, whispered nervously to Hi that the woman "looked just like Eva Perón."

Learning nothing he didn't already know, Hi decided to call it a night and start with a clear head in the morning. Intending to hail a taxi, Hi went outside Cuco's. But the midnight fog, which seemed almost supernatural, was so thick Hi could hardly see the sidewalk in front of him, much less any passing taxi.

Hi walked east on Corrientes in the fog. As he did, he began hearing footsteps behind him. Crossing Calle Florida (a pedestrian street—no taxi here), he kept walking. He should have gone west, toward Nueve de Julio, but he mistakenly thought the Plaza de Mayo was not far away down east Corrientes. There he could get a taxi to Recoleta and his rented bungalow. But the plaza was blocks to the south. And soon east Corrientes, as he walked, was deserted.

Those footsteps behind him continued, not too far

away in the fog. They seemed to stop whenever Hi did. He determined to find out who it was—and to not let himself get knocked out again. Hi stepped into a doorway and waited.

The footsteps approached. Hi took a deep breath, the adrenalin pumping, and stepped out from the fog-shrouded doorway. He almost scared Soto to death. Looking into his face, Hi remembered seeing this man, who had reacted self-consciously, both nights in the cabaret.

Soto tried to turn away, but Hi grabbed him by his pinstriped lapel. "Stick around, pal," Hi said. "What's your name?"

Soto quickly reached into his coat. Hi, figuring he was going for a gun, caught the man with a right to the jaw, knocking Soto out cold.

Kneeling down, Hi began searching the man's coat. "Something weird's going on, pal," Hi said, as if Soto could hear, "and I'll bet you know something about it." Hi found a loaded .38 inside the coat. Hi stuck the gun under his own belt, then found Soto's wallet and opened it. A condom fell out, which Hi left on the sidewalk. Hi looked at the man's driver's license. Under NAME it said, "Hernán Soto." Under OCCUPATION it said, "None of Your Business."

As Hi pocketed the wallet, he heard a car, and headlights appeared in the fog. To Hi's relief, it was a taxi that stopped by the curb.

"Good to see you," Hi cheerfully told the driver, a heavyset, blackheaded fellow with a pencil moustache and a very concerned look on his face. "My buddy's passed out. I was trying to get him to the plaza."

"What plaza?"

"Help me get the drunkard home."

The driver got out to help Hi lift his unconscious friend into the taxi.

10

Ministry of Blood

AS KEGEL TRUDGED TO GEBÄUDE VIER in the moonlight, he cursed the jungle for the thousandth time. It wasn't the temperature that was so enervating—tonight it was but 70 degrees Fahrenheit—it was that 85-percent relative humidity. What price glory, Kegel thought, what a test of one's will. He could sure use a glass of cold blood.

Entering Gebäude Vier, Kegel headed down the central corridor, lit only by kerosene wall lamps. On the right were doors leading to the Wasserkontrollzimmer and the deadly indoor Pfuhl. Kegel continued to a door on the left, which took him into the blood extraction unit: a stark, smelly chamber that bore no resemblance to a Weinberg (Vineyard), which is what the unit was officially called.

Sturmbannführer (Lieutenant-Colonel) Frankel, seated at his desk, quickly rose as Kegel entered the dimly lit unit. Dorsch had voiced suspicion that Frankel was pilfering blood, and tonight, Kegel noted, the Sturmbannführer looked as well-fed as ever. But if Frankel was pilfering, he never left any bloodstains, nor drank enough to make a measurable difference. At most he was just wetting his palate.

"Sturmbannführer, how is production?" Kegel asked.

"Very good, Obergruppenführer. All except for . . ." Frankel looked quickly at a document on his desk. "Number three. A bad case of anemia."

"Another stingy one, eh?" Kegel said with ironic pleasure. "Mark him down for conversion."

"Right away, sir."

"Let's bill him for Saturday night." Turning toward the row of cells, Kegel glanced back at a paper-littered desk behind Frankel's. "Where is Oberschütze Spitz?"

"Gone for more syringes," Frankel said, taking a flashlight from his desk. "We just had to quiet one down."

Kegel and Frankel began moving along the dark row of cells that housed the raw blood supply, Frankel shining the flashlight. An assortment of captives—explorers, tourists, Amazon natives—occupied primitive individual cells. Some were at that very moment having blood extracted, by a remotely controlled system of needles, tubes, and pipes, while others, the needles never leaving their arms, languished on bunks between their regularly scheduled donations. They languished in darkness, for the Nazis were not about to expend gasoline, kerosene, or candles to give these poor souls some light. The remote control was a perverse innovation that sharply contrasted with the otherwise Stone Age nature of the Weinberg.

Explorer Crowley, as the Nazis came by his cell, looked up weakly from his bunk. "Hey, what about my partner?" he demanded to know. "What have you done with him?"

Kegel smiled through the bars at Crowley. "He has been converted. How is my English?"

"It stinks," Crowley said, squinting in the beam of the flashlight. " 'Converted?' "

"Yes. And what about you?" Kegel asked, ignoring Crowley's insult. "Would you like a dip in our pool?"

Crowley didn't know what that meant, but it sounded basically terminal. "Doesn't sound too inviting," he muttered.

"Then you have to keep giving," Kegel urged. "You must keep eating well."

"Eating well?" Crowley asked, almost laughing.

"Keep that blood pressure up. Keep producing fresh blood. We have a nice saying here: 'A few drops a day keep piranhas away.' "

Kegel chortled as he left Crowley's cell.

Next door to the Weinberg was the blood storage unit, or Weinkellar. The blood extracted in the Weinberg cells was piped directly into this unit, to be bottled and refrigerated till consumed. In the Weinkellar also was the cubby-hole office of Obersturmbannführer (Colonel) Müller, whom Kegel stopped by to see—though Müller never had much to say. The Weinberg and Weinkellar comprised, under Müller, the mystically named Ministerium von Elixir von der Ewiger Rebstock ("Ministry of Elixir from the Eternal Vine") or MEER ("sea" in German). In short, Müller was in charge of all blood. After Kegel he was the leanest, and after the Führer and Kegel the meanest, man on the compound. Frankel or anyone else would think twice before pilfering blood from Obersturmbannführer Müller.

As Kegel left Gebäude Vier, he again cursed the jungle. Dorsch was right, he concluded. He must speak with the Führer. The rest of Hitler's memoirs could wait. Did not the Führer's best years lie ahead? Dorsch was right, too, about Señora Perón. But that was best left alone: to them, as Dorsch said, she meant nothing. What mattered was that all their plans start moving ahead. Time was of the essence, though they had all the time in the world. For any day now the world might discover them. And surely it would seek their destruction.

11

The Man from IQ

THE TAXI DRIVER couldn't wait to be rid of this fare. He had never had a fight break out in the back seat of his taxi before. Soto had awakened, a struggle had ensued, and Hi had been obliged to knock the guy out again. "He's one rowdy drunk," Hi told the driver.

They reached the small bungalow Hi rented in Recoleta, an upper-class suburb northwest from downtown BA. The driver parked the taxi behind a black 1952 Chevy sedan that sat at the curb in the fog. In the taxi's headlight beams Hi could see the backs of two heads in the Chevy. When the taxi driver started to get out, Hi, warily watching the Chevy's occupants, said, "Stay put. Be ready to get our butts out of here."

"Are they going to try to kill you?" asked the suddenly scared driver.

"Who knows?" Hi said, his hand on the gun in his belt. "They may try to sell me some encyclopedias."

They watched two men get out of the Chevy. Hi was relieved to recognize one as Diego. "Relax, pal," Hi told the driver. "False alarm."

Hi got out and smiled at Diego. "Hello, compadre. Give me a hand." Diego and McKay began helping Hi get the deadweight Soto out of the taxi.

"Who is it?" Diego asked.

"That's what I intend to find out."

"I thought he was your friend," snapped the taxi driver, now certain he was an accomplice in something.

"I was lying," Hi said as he paid him. "Keep the change." The driver wasted no time driving off.

At the front door Hi took out his key, Diego and McKay toting Soto by his arms and feet. "What brings you to BA?" Hi asked Diego.

"Adolf Hitler."

Hi looked quizzically at McKay.

"My name is McKay. You and I need to talk."

"He works for IQ," said Diego, as Hi unlocked the door.

"Too bad, I don't have any IQ to spare," Hi quipped. "Bring in the garbage, will ya?"

House rentals in BA were not easy to find, and Hi, wanting a place to himself, had had to rent on short notice. He had given the address to Diego, who now found it to be a small but tastefully furnished place, with what would be a fine view, on clear nights, from its patio. Diego and McKay dumped the still-unconscious Soto onto the couch, while Hi, from what had become pure habit, walked over to the bar. But Hi would have this drink in celebration, not despair. He knew that Eva, whether or not she might ever again be his, was alive. "What'll you have, Diego?" he asked, pouring himself a scotch.

"Got an RC?"

"Bought 'em right down the street. McKay?"

"Something with pisco. Good stuff."

Hi sighed and looked over at Diego. "Tell him he's not in Peru."

"Sorry," said the Britisher, realizing his mistake. "Then give me, uh . . . "

"You're drinking some scotch," Hi said, pouring it. "Now what's this about—Adolf Hitler?" Hi wanted to get this over with. I've got to figure out how to find Eva, he thought, and this guy wants to talk about the war?

McKay, noting Soto wake up, said, "I'm not sure our friend here should hear it."

Soto, sitting up on the couch, looked curiously around. Hi, handing McKay his scotch, walked over to Soto as he got to his feet. Grabbing Soto by the lapel with one hand, Hi knocked him out with the other. As Soto fell back on the couch, Hi took Soto's pistol from his belt and handed it to Diego. "Keep him covered. I'll get your RC." On his way back to the bar, Hi glanced impatiently at McKay. "I'm waiting." Diego had never seen Hi so hyper.

McKay briefly filled Hi in on IQ, then reached into a coat pocket and produced a small photograph. He walked over to Hi, who had just finished pouring a bottle of RC over ice, and handed him the black-and-white photo.

"Countess Borca of Romania," McKay said as Hi looked at her singular image. "Transylvania, to be exact."

"Transylvania? I could have guessed," Hi said with amusement, having read *Dracula* twice. "She looks like a vampire."

"She is," McKay said. "Or was." Hi looked at him incredulously. "She was the talk of Transylvania."

Hi studied McKay's eyes, which calmly gazed back. Hi looked over at Diego, who innocently shrugged. "Can I have my RC?" Diego asked.

After glancing again at the photo, Hi handed it back to McKay. Maybe the lady was a vampire and maybe she wasn't. To hell with it. "What's she got to do with the Führer?" Hi asked, delivering the RC to Diego.

"In 1944," McKay said, "she was taken into custody and flown to Berlin by Hitler's elite guard, the SS."

Soto, waking up again, got unsteadily to his feet. Diego walked over and knocked him out.

"I suppose you're going to tell me," Hi said to McKay, "that the Führer had this lady put the bite on him."

"Exactly. For the Führer, to become a vampire was to become immortal. Losing the war would be losing one battle. He would live to fight again."

"Where is he now?"

"Somewhere in the Amazon jungle. We know he has contacted several South American leaders. His aim is to rule, first South America, then the world, through bribery: by offering world leaders something far more precious than power or gold. Immortality."

Hi considered for a moment, then shook his head skeptically. He had seen a good deal of that jungle, and there weren't any WW2 German Nazis around. The ones he knew of were all in suburbia. (He made a mental note: make a list for IQ.) "You've got to be kidding," Hi said.

"His first South American contact," said McKay, "was Argentina's Juan Domingo Perón."

Hi felt a chill shoot straight down his spine. "Wait a minute," he said, too quickly. He got some scotch down his windpipe and coughed. Suddenly, frighteningly, McKay's story had taken on a whole new complexion. "Did this involve Eva?" Hi struggled to ask, his eyes watering from the fumes in his lungs.

"You okay?" asked Diego. Hi nodded yes, but coughed wetly, and yanked out a handkerchief for his running nose.

"We know," McKay said, "that Eva Perón traveled, as her husband's emissary, to Hitler's secret jungle headquarters." Now Hi couldn't stop coughing. "She never returned." Hi thought he was going to strangle. "According to our Argentine sources . . ." Hi reeled toward the bathroom. ". . . Perón believes she fell for the Führer." Hi bent over the commode and threw up.

McKay and Diego waited. Hi came back out, over the coughing but breathing heavily, wiping his tearing eyes, trying to clear his throat. "And became a vampire?" he croaked. McKay was not even sure what Hi asked.

"She became a vampire?" Diego repeated to McKay.

"That would seem likely," McKay said, tactfully answering what he thought a dumb question. "The deserted Perón had little choice but to fake an untimely death for his beloved Evita. How else to explain her absence?"

"That's not her body in the ministry," Hi admitted, still recovering his voice. "You're right about that." Hi looked at puzzled Diego. "I saw her tonight, Diego. In downtown BA."

Diego thought for a moment. "Then has she left Hitler?" he speculated. "Can she go back to Perón?" He looked at McKay. "If it's true what you say," Diego told him, "then between Perón and the Führer there must now be . . . how else to say it? Bad blood."

"True," McKay said. "Perón, I am sure, wants Hitler dead." McKay looked at Hi. "But then don't we all."

Hi braved another sip of scotch. "That's where I come in?"

"No other man in the world knows the Amazon jungle as well as you," McKay said. "You're the logical choice to help lead a special team." Looking Hi straight in the eye, McKay spoke with all the conviction he could muster. "We must destroy him, destroy, before it starts, his vampire empire. We must save the world from Hitler Part Two."

Hi shook his head in wonder. It was almost too much to believe. "I sure thought we had him at the end of Part One."

Soto woke up. This time he was not so quick to rise from the couch. He watched warily as Hi walked over to him.

"Okay, friend," Hi said in Spanish, "you've got some explaining to do."

"Speak in English," said McKay, whose Spanish was

not very good. Hi looked at him irritably. McKay added, "*Por favor.*"

Hi took out the wallet he had taken from Soto, who cautiously got to his feet. Hi asked him in English, "You speak English?"

"Maybe I do," Soto said uncooperatively in English, "and maybe I don't."

Hi began examining the wallet's contents as Soto resentfully watched. "Hernán Soto," Hi read from the driver's license. "What else have we got here?"

Soto stood at Hi's shoulder and began pointing out photos in the wallet. "This is my wife Carlota. My three-year-old daughter—"

Hi slapped away Soto's hand. "Who do you work for?" Hi demanded. "Why were you tailing me?"

Soto was defiant. "I have nothing to say," he replied.

"Yeah? We'll see about that."

"What shall we do?" asked Diego, ready and willing to assist.

"Tie him up, gag him," Hi said, tossing the wallet aside. "We'll put him in the closet for a couple of days. Maybe that'll loosen his tongue."

"What do we tie him with?" asked McKay.

Looking around, Hi pointed to a table lamp. "Use the cord off that lamp. The damn thing doesn't work anyway."

While Diego and McKay set to work, Hi got them a roll of adhesive tape he had bought to pack some mementos, including a nice bust of Eva, that he had impulsively picked up that day. He then poured himself some more scotch and walked out onto the patio. The patio's view, he thought, would help him relax and think, though there was nothing to look at but fog.

12

A Visit from Wolfgang

DIEGO AND MCKAY sat Soto, bound with cord, mouth taped, on the floor of the closet. "Have a nice evening," said Diego, with McKay adding, "Stay out of trouble." Diego closed the door, which McKay then jammed by propping a chair under the latch.
    Diego and McKay joined Hi on the patio. Hi, sipping his scotch, stood gazing into the zero visibility.
    "Well, what do you say?" asked McKay.
    Hi replied rhetorically, "Do I want to help you go in and kill Hitler?"
    "Him and his vampire henchmen. We don't know how many."
    "I'd do it with relish. But what about Eva?"
    "If Eva is with him," Diego said, "what is she doing in Buenos Aires? That is, if it was really her you saw."
    "I saw her, Diego," Hi said, with no doubt in his mind.
    McKay sighed. He had no ready answer for the Eva complication. "It's been a long day, we're all tired," said the man from IQ. He turned to Diego. "Let's get back to the hotel and turn in." Then he looked again at Hi. "We'll talk more in the morning."
    A few hours later Hi was snoring away on the couch. He hadn't made it to the bedroom, after finishing off the bottle of scotch. Hi was dreaming of Eva—the dream was weird and disjointed—when there appeared on the fog-

covered patio, about four in the morning, a large, black, lumbering bat.

Hi's dream became more chaotic, a phantasmagoria of beastly, frightening images. Then Hi drifted into a state of semiconsciousness, in which a hulking, shadowy figure seemed to approach and lurk over him. Then Hi realized he was no longer dreaming. Springing off the couch to his feet, he found himself face-to-face with the smirking oaf who had slugged him when he tried to chase Eva.

This time it was Hi who struck first, slamming a fist into the intruder's hard midriff. The only effect of the blow was a sharp pain in Hi's hand. Hi grabbed the empty scotch bottle off the table by the couch and smashed it over the oaf's blonde, closely cropped head. The intruder just smiled, then grabbed Hi by his shirt and belt.

"What's your name, pal?" Hi asked.

"Wolfgang," he said, lifting Hi off the floor. Wolfgang effortlessly threw Hi over the couch and into the wall behind it.

Wolfgang then proceeded to tear up most of the furniture, using Hi's vainly resisting body as the instrument of destruction.

Crashing into an end table with a drawer in it, Hi remembered that he had stashed Soto's pistol there. He snatched the gun out of the drawer and fired three bullets into the incredibly powerful ogre standing over him. Seeing the shots had no effect, Hi tossed the gun aside, saying, "That's what I figured."

Eluding Wolfgang's grasp, Hi, with the last of his strength, grabbed up a fireplace poker, only to have the hulk easily wrest it from him. Throwing Hi to the floor, Wolfgang got down over him with the poker, which he held—against the weakening resistance of Hi's hand round his wrist—as if to plunge it down into Hi's neck.

Exhausted, Hi lay there waiting to die, his arm losing all power to resist the poker being pressed down over him. But Wolfgang, smiling smugly down at Hi as he held him pinned to the floor, then relaxed the pressure. Wolfgang was not going to kill him.

"What's holding you back?" Hi asked, with hardly the breath to say it.

"Señora Perón," the monster said calmly. "I am here to take you to her."

Hi couldn't believe his ears. "You had to wreck this place first?"

Wolfgang kept smiling. "I don't like being hit with a bottle."

13

Eva—Warts and All

A SINGLE LAMP BURNED in the secluded mansion's study where Eva sat waiting, morose and alone, in a fresh black suit. Crushing out a cigarette, she rose from her high-backed padded chair at the sound outside of an arriving car. Concerned about her upswept hair, she walked over to a mirror, forgetting, till she got there, that she had no reflection. Frustratedly adjusting one of her earrings, which had small wooden pendants, she returned to the chair, sat down, and nervously lit a fresh cigarette. Sitting back and crossing her legs, she struck a calm pose.

After a minute or so, the door of the study opened, and Hi walked in. Wolfgang, remaining outside in the hallway, closed the door. For a moment, Hi and Eva just looked at each other. Hi's heart ached, but he didn't let on.

"Hello, Hi."

"Hello, Eva." Hi took a padded chair facing Eva's across the room. "What brings you out of the jungle?"

Eva was impressed. "You know that much already?"

"Yeah. A little bat told me. Just visiting?"

"Yes. I got homesick." She took a drag from the cigarette. "It was such a surprise to run into you."

"*You* were surprised?" He watched her lovely lips blow out the smoke. "You ought to quit smoking. It'll shorten your life."

"How did you quit?"

"I took up drinking instead." Hi nodded toward the closed door. "Who's the clown you've got with you?"

"His name is Wolfgang."

"So he claims."

"SS. He is assigned to protect me. I hope he didn't hurt you."

"Nah." Hi fidgeted in his chair, not because he was nervous but because he was in excruciating physical pain. "We just worked out together."

"What are you doing in Argentina? So far from lost cities."

"I'm here for the funeral. Haven't you heard? You're dead. Everybody's in mourning."

"You must forget about me. Life must go on."

"They even fooled me with the body. The first time. But then, after you gave me the slip, I went back and saw it."

"Saw what?"

"They forgot the little wart." He watched her instinctively touch a tiny wart just below her right jaw. Hi sadly shook his head. "Nobody's perfect. But you were so close."

Hi got up from his chair. He was mad now, began pacing. "You fell for the Führer?" he asked accusingly.

"Not really. He did the falling." Eva sighed. "I was so sick of Juan. Then I met the Führer. He offered me immortal power."

"Pretty hard to turn down," Hi cracked cynically. "Eva, you're really on a power kick."

"I was. I should have stuck with the soaps. And you. But I did do some good for my country. Till I met *him*."

"What happened to his first Eva? Braun."

"He left her in the bunker in Berlin."

"Nice guy."

"She didn't want to be a vampire. Smart move."

"You can't be in love with him. Can you?"

"Of course not. I'm ashamed to be with him." She

tensely crushed out her cigarette. "It was the mother of all mistakes."

"How can you go back to him?"

"What choice do I have?" she said loudly, then glanced at the door, suspecting that Wolfgang was listening behind it. She sighed, then rose from her chair to pace too, speaking quietly again. "Do you think Adolf would let me leave and not return?" She gestured toward the door. "Do you think he sends Wolfgang *only* to protect me? No." Eva paused despairingly. There were tears in her eyes. "There is no other place for me. Not now."

She was standing by a painting on the wall. She wistfully regarded the portrait. It was of an Argentine gaucho, though the face was John Wayne's. "It's just that I had to see Argentina."

"Maybe get a little Argentine blood?"

Eva turned to him. He saw the hurt in her eyes. "Sorry," he said softly.

"Do you think for an instant I enjoy it?"

"Hell, you might as well try."

They looked at each other for a moment.

"Don't come after us, Hi. Please."

"Concerned for my health?"

"Yes." She smiled sadly. "I didn't stop loving you when I married Juan."

"You might as well have."

"And you didn't stop loving me."

"No, I didn't."

"Can I kiss you goodbye?"

She walked over to him. They gazed into each other's eyes, then her lips moved toward his.

"Just don't go for the neck," Hi whispered.

As they enjoyed a lingering kiss, Hi half-opened his eyes, to be sure he was right about something. Yes, she was wearing vilca-wood earrings. Hi knew where he had seen those before.

Their lips parted. Eva looked at him lovingly, said goodbye, and walked out of the room.

Wolfgang again blindfolded Hi for the ride back to town. As Wolfgang drove the car into the outskirts of BA, day was breaking.

"You can take off the blindfold," the Nazi told Hi, sitting in the right front seat. "We are in Buenos Aires."

Hi took off the blindfold, and was surprised to see daylight. He looked over at Wolfgang. "Shouldn't you be in a coffin somewhere?"

Wolfgang chuckled. "You have seen too many Dracula films. Vampires can function all hours."

Hi studied him. "But not at full strength. That's why you're night people. No supernatural powers in the daytime. Right?"

Wolfgang shrugged. "We have powers, but diminished. Have *you* ever stayed up for twenty-four hours?"

"Yeah. It's a draining experience." Hi shook his head with amazement. "You know, Wolfie, you're pretty dumb. Driving into town with me sitting here wearing a blindfold. Don't you think folks might get suspicious?" Hi then pretended to catch on. "I get it. You're only dumb in the day."

For a moment Wolfgang drove silently, sulking. Then he blew out a sigh of frustration. "Señora Perón is a fool. You know too much. She ought to let me kill you."

"Tough talk. Right now, Wolfie, in the full light of day, I bet I could take you."

Wolfgang looked at Hi as if inviting him to try.

"Lucky for you," Hi added, "I've got too much else to go do."

"What have you got to do?" Wolfgang asked.

"I've got a damn house to clean up."

14

Soto Has To Go

HI LOOKED at the busted furniture with disgust. "I'll never rent in *this* town again," he said to no one. Then he remembered that someone was there.

Hi opened the closet and knelt down by the bound, sweat-drenched Soto, who grunted urgently behind the tape on his mouth.

"Okay, pal, time's up," Hi said in English, taking hold of a corner of the tape. "You better be ready to talk." With a jerk Hi ripped off the tape, yanking hairs by the roots out of Soto's moustache. "What have you got to say?"

Soto howled in searing pain.

"Is that all?"

Soto was beside himself. "I need to use el baño," he said pleadingly.

"Oh, no," Hi said as if talking to a child, "el baño for Soto's a no-no."

"Then kill me!"

Hi obligingly went to look for the pistol. He found it lying under the couch, which as a result of Wolfgang's visit had only two intact legs. Someone knocked at the front door. "It's open!" Hi shouted.

Walking in, Diego and McKay were taken aback by the damage.

"Morning, guys," Hi said with a wink, being sure that Soto could hear. "You're just in time for the fireworks."

Diego and McKay followed Hi to the closet. Hi got down before Soto and stuck the muzzle of the pistol to the desperate man's sweat-dripping nose.

"Here you go, Soto," Hi said cheerily, "to that great el baño below. *Uno.* I'll bet you can't wait. *Dos.*" Hi cocked the hammer. "*Tres.*"

"Wait!" Soto shouted.

Hi waited, leaning forward to hear. The rattled Soto glanced up at McKay. "Your English friend," he said reluctantly. "Who does he work for?"

"What's it to you?" Hi said.

Soto glanced again at McKay. "Let me out, untie me," he said resignedly. "I will tell you. *After* I use el baño."

Untied, Soto spent about ten minutes alone in the bathroom. Besides using the toilet he drank about a gallon of water from the tap. Hi and the others patiently waited, knowing that the john had no window and Soto could hardly escape through the plumbing. Soto came out a different man, calm and relaxed, though still soggy from his stay in the closet.

"I work for the Argentine government," Soto volunteered, as Hi handed him back his wallet.

"How high in the government?" asked Hi.

"El Presidente Perón."

Hi and the others exchanged glances. "You've been following me under orders from Perón?"

"My instructions were to see who may contact you," Soto said, checking the contents of his wallet. "If it were someone from the Intelligence Quorum, it could only mean one thing."

"What's that?" asked McKay.

"How should I know?" Soto said irritably. "I am quoting Perón." Soto pocketed his wallet.

"So what are you supposed to do now?" Hi asked,

handing Soto his gun.

Glancing at McKay, Soto returned the .38 to his coat. "Before you do anything with or for this man," he told Hi, "I must take you to La Casa Rosada. El Presidente wishes to see you."

15

The Pink House Blues

JUAN DOMINGO PERÓN sat alone in his Casa Rosada (Pink House) office. His business suit was immaculate, his black hair neatly plastered, but the six-foot, slightly paunchy, fifty-seven-year-old president wasn't busy with affairs of state. He sat slouched, his back to the door, in his high-backed swivel chair, his watery eyes on a framed 8 by 10 picture of Eva. The picture was on the cabinet of a hi-fi record player behind Juan's desk. A 78-rpm record was playing, the president morosely listening. The song was "Counting the Ways." It had been their song, his and Eva's, and it was almost overwhelming to hear.

> *I'm not counting the ways*
> *That I'm crazy for you—*
> *You'd be amazed,*
> *It's more than I can do.*
> *If I counted the ways*
> *That I love and adore you*
> *For the rest of my days,*
> *I could never get through.*

The office door opened, and a prim, middle-aged presidential assistant named Martínez brought in Hi in his freshly pressed three-piece suit. The president, lost in the music and memories, was not even aware of their entrance. Hi, hearing "Counting the Ways," thought Juan had some kind of nerve. Eva had sung it—the one song she knew in rote English—at Cuco's. It had become their song, hers and Hi's. Hi felt like taking the 78 and busting it over Juan's head.

Martínez politely said, "Mr. President—"

"Leave me alone," Juan snapped without as much as a glance at Martínez.

"Mr. Hickenlooper is here."

"I am not to be disturbed." Juan then realized what name he had heard. "Wait!" he said, turning his chair. "Did you say—"

"Hickenlooper."

"Why didn't you say so?" Juan quickly rose to turn off the music. As Martínez left, closing the door, Juan, chin up, chest swollen, strode forward to greet Hi. "So! Mr.—eh..."

"Hickenlooper," Hi prompted him.

"Yes." They shook hands, Juan using a viselike grip that would crush a child's bones. I *hate* guys who do that, Hi thought.

"My condolences," Hi said.

"One must take Eva's death like a man," Juan said firmly. He motioned Hi to a chair in front of the desk.

"That song you were playing," Hi said as he stepped to the chair, Juan heading back to his. "I've heard it many times."

They sat down. "It was our song," Juan said.

"Yeah? Ours too."

Juan was taken aback. "That song gets around."

"Seventy-eight revolutions per minute."

Juan regarded his guest for a moment. "You still love her," Juan said. Hi didn't know how to respond. "Let us speak frankly," Juan urged. "Man to man. We are machos."

"Yeah," Hi said, "I still love her."

"Who doesn't?" Juan declared. "Who could fall out of love with Evita? No one. Not even Juan Perón."

Hi smiled lamely. "You're a regular guy, Mr. President."

Juan beamed appreciatively. Then abruptly he turned very grave. "Tell me, Mr.—eh..." Hi just looked at him. "Hickenlooper," Juan got it right. "How much do you know?" Hi shifted uncomfortably in his chair. "Speak freely, please," Juan said encouragingly. "Macho to macho."

Hi cleared his throat. "Well," he began, "I know that you made a pact with the devil." Juan was stunned. "Adolf Hitler." Juan's eyes lost their focus. "At least you intended to." Juan's mouth hung open, his lower lip trembled. "Until he stole your wife."

Juan burst into tears. "The body at the ministry isn't Eva's," Hi continued. Juan shook his head no, his body shaking with sobs. "Her last appearances, during her supposed illness," Hi said, "were performed by a double." Juan nodded yes as he wailed. "Did the double know," Hi asked accusingly, "that dying would be a part of the job?" Sobbing Juan shook his head no, the accusation not even registering. "Anything to save face, eh, Mr. President? Even murder."

That got Juan's attention. Suddenly there were knocks at the door, which got Juan's attention too. Juan quickly rose, wiping his eyes, and turned to be facing the window as Martínez walked in with a document. "Mr. President—"

"Yes," Juan said impatiently, not turning around.

"Excuse me for interrupting your thoughts," said Martínez, stepping to the front of the desk. "I must have your signature before this document can be delivered."

Juan turned, grabbed a pen, as Martínez placed the

document on the desk. Leaning over it, Juan scribbled his signature, without looking up at Martínez. "Can't you think of these things at the appropriate time?" Juan complained. He tossed the pen on the desk as he turned again to the window.

"I am sorry, sir," said Martínez as he picked up the document. "Please forgive the intrusion."

Martínez quickly left, closing the door.

Juan was convulsed by a sob. Turning from the window, he grabbed the back of the desk chair with one hand for support. "It is true what you say," he sniveled. He began moving around the desk toward Hi. "What a fool I was, to consider getting mixed up with Hitler." Tears rolled down the president's cheeks. "What a fool, worst of all, to involve Evita . . . "

Juan fell to his knees before Hi.

" . . . To let her be taken to his lair." Juan crawled closer to his fascinated guest. "I should never have let her go," he whined. He clutched Hi's knee, pressed his cheek to it, wetting Hi's pants leg with tears. "He stole my Evita. You must help me get her back. You love her as I do."

Juan groveled more, began clinging to Hi's lower leg. "You know what's like to lose her," he blubbered, Hi barely able to understand him. "Please. Please, Mr. Hucklelucker."

Juan was lying on the floor now, wailing, hugging Hi's ankle, wetting the shoe on Hi's clubfoot.

There were knocks, the door opened, Juan quickly crawling away from Hi. Martínez entered, document in hand, to find Juan on all fours.

"Mr. President, what is wrong?" asked the startled aide.

"What does it look like, you fool?" Juan said with disdain. "I've lost something on the floor."

"May I help you find it, sir?" Martínez asked, wondering why Hi just sat in his chair with detachment.

"You don't even know what to look for," Juan said, as he went crawling behind his desk. "What do you want now?"

"I forgot, sir," the flustered aide said as he took the document to the desk, "that you must sign in two places."

Juan, trying to rise behind the desk, banged his head under the edge of the knee well. He got up holding his head.

"Mr. President, I will summon the doctor," Martínez said urgently.

"It's all right," Juan said through clenched teeth.

"But, sir, you are crying in pain."

"It's all right!" Juan bellowed. Grabbing the pen, he again scribbled his signature. "Is there a third place I should sign, you lunatic?"

"No, sir," Martínez said. "I am sorry."

The aide quickly left. Juan took a moment to compose himself. Hi patiently sat, contemplating his wet knee.

"So," Juan said. "You have been contacted by the Intelligence Quorum. That can only mean one thing."

"I hope you're not quoting Soto," Hi said.

"They want your assistance," Juan observed, "in locating Hitler and his vampire colony." He picked up a thin, white, lettersize envelope from the desk. "I assume they intend to destroy him."

"That's about the size of it."

"Destroying a bunch of vampires will be no easy task." Juan was moving, envelope in hand, around the desk toward Hi.

"Especially Nazi ones," Hi said, his eyes on the envelope. "They're the worst."

"I wish to help," Juan said, as he stopped in front of

Hi. "But there is the question, of course, of Evita." One hand idly tapped the other with the envelope. "She must somehow be saved. We must help her."

"I'm with you on that," Hi said, getting up from his chair. "But how?" He wondered what was in that envelope.

"There is a hematologist, a blood doctor," Juan explained, turning the envelope over, then over again, though it was blank on both sides, "who for the past several months has been engaged in research, using vampire bats"—he held the envelope on five fingertips as if weighing it—"not only to find a possible cure"—he cleaned a fingernail with a corner of the envelope, though his nails were immaculate—"but to discover how a host of vampires might best be destroyed." He held the envelope up to the light. "He is on the verge, he believes, of success."

"May I have the envelope *please*," Hi said.

Juan hesitated, then handed it over. "His name is Chou Po," Juan said. "You have in your hand the directions you need. Call him first. Use the code name Dracaena."

"Dracaena," Hi repeated. "I'll call Doctor Po right away. Thanks a lot." Hi pocketed the envelope.

They walked toward the door, Juan with a hand on Hi's shoulder. "Let me know," Juan said, "if I may be of further assistance. Just be certain, my friend, whatever the final plan of action"—Juan bit his lip, becoming emotional again, as they reached the closed door—"that Evita is not harmed."

"It's like you said, Mr. President, I love her too," Hi assured him. "I've got her welfare in mind."

Juan broke down again, clutching Hi's shoulder. "Then please," he said, "please bring her back."

"She knows she made a mistake," Hi said. "She sees no way out."

"Bring her back to me," Juan pleaded, his eyes like two bad faucets, dripping tears on Hi's coat. "Bring back our Evita."

Hi opened the door, trying politely to free himself, sobbing Juan clinging to him, pressing his forehead to Hi's shoulder. Where does he get all those tears? Hi wondered. From his bladder? "I'll save her, Mr. President. Don't worry."

"Yes, save her, please," weeping Juan begged, not wanting to let go of Hi. "Kill Hitler, kill them all, but save Evita. Bring her back—"

"Goodbye, Mr. President."

Hi slipped free, closing the door behind him. Juan put his forehead against the door as he sobbed.

There were knocks, Martínez quickly opened the door. It knocked out Juan Domingo Perón.

16

Doctor Po

"THE DRACAENA palm," said Chou Po, an amiable, first-generation Chinese hematologist who also knew his botany. Diminutive in his white lab coat, the forty-one-year-old Po was introducing Hi, Diego, and McKay to the same leafy, red-flowered plant species that once decorated Castle Borca in Romania.

Po and his visitors were in a fairly goodsized laboratory adjoining Po's office. Beakers on a counter contained dark red liquid that Hi and his friends assumed to be blood. The Dracaena, with the help of the small square table on which it sat, stood higher than Po did, and was not quite like anything in the plant line that Hi and the others recalled seeing.

"The name is from Greek," Po said. "Dracaena means dragon, or devil." He gently lifted for display one of the large red blooms. "The flower is much like a rose." He then drew their attention to the Dracaena palm's stem, about the size of a quarter in circumference. "By the first, oh, one hundred and twenty days, the young plant develops, right here in the stem, a red-colored liquid, called appropriately dragon's blood."

"That's nice to know, Doctor Po," Hi said with impatience, "but what's this Dracaena got to do with vampires?"

"There is a legend," the smiling Po said, "that the

ancient Greeks named this plant in the vampire's honor." He began walking toward a closed door. "That is why vampires—so some believe—like to keep this palm in their homes, as a decorative plant." Po chuckled as he stopped by the door. "If only they knew."

"Knew what?" Hi asked.

"The nature of the plant's red secretion." Po opened the door as the others walked over. The door led to a small lab room with counters and cabinets. "In researching, I asked myself: Is there a particular reason why the Greeks would name this plant for the vampire?" The lights within the room were off, so that Hi, Diego, and McKay, as they peered through the door past Po, were unsure of what they saw on a table in the middle of the room. Po motioned for them to follow him in. "Why, besides color," he continued, "might this liquid be called dragon's blood?"

Po turned on the lights as his three guests entered the small lab room. "The answer is here," he said, as his visitors peered with wonder at the thing on the table. "The liquid was named, not for its bloodlike appearance, but for its effect upon blood." The three visitors moved for a closer look. "Dragon's blood," Po added for effect. "The blood of the devil."

They were looking at a vampire bat. It was hanging upside down, as bats are wont to do, from a perch on the table. The bat was tethered to the perch by one leg. Vampire bats, with their snouts, fangs, and small piercing eyes, were always ugly in pictures, and Po's visitors, looking at the real thing, could see why.

"The Desmodonidas," Po said. "Do not worry. He is tied, he cannot attack you." He then informed Hi, "When you called, about one half hour ago, I chose this bat to show you. I had fed it, with liquid extracted from the palm, about five and a half hours ago." Po glanced at his watch.

"In another half hour, it will happen."
"What will?" Hi asked.
"The destruction of the vampire. How ironic, you see, that any vampire would keep such a plant. I have written a poem:

*When vampires smell their Dracaena palm roses,
The seeds of destruction are under their noses.*"

"Look!" said Diego, staring at the bat.
It had begun shaking and smoking. Blood was seeping, then began pouring, out of its body openings.
"It has already started," Po said with surprise. "It is early."
"What's happening?" Hi asked, as they watched the bat smoke, shake, and bleed.
"The extract is a powerful coagulant," Po explained. "There is violent chemical reaction, clotting the blood, the vampire hemorrhages. Horribly. Sometimes it even explodes."
The bat exploded, splattering them all with blood and bits of flesh. Hi's three-piece suit, already tearstained, was ruined.
Po smiled a bit sheepishly. "Which is why it pays to wear a lab coat," he added.
As Po and his guests washed up at the main laboratory's sinks, McKay nodded toward one of the beakers of dragon's blood. "That extract," McKay said, "is utterly impractical."
"How so?" asked the doctor.
"The time required. You kill a vampire with a stake through the heart. That doesn't take six hours."
"Five hours and a half," Hi corrected him wryly.
"It was the first time it has happened so soon," Po said,

as if that really mattered.

"It works with bats, Doctor Po," Hi said, "but what about humans?"

"I cannot be certain," Po replied, "with no human vampires to work on."

"Bats are mammals," said Diego, drying his face. "So are humans."

"Yes," Po said. "So the effect is possibly similar."

"How much extract would it take?" Hi asked, dropping his bloodstained coat and vest in the garbage.

"For humans? Quite a lot. You would need, I would say, one plant, at least four months old, for every three or four humans, to get them to hemorrhage."

"Like I said: impractical," said McKay, wiping bat debris off a shoe.

"How about the cure, Doc?" Hi asked. "Perón said you're onto a vampire cure."

"Oh yes, the cure," Po said, smiling. "I cannot be sure of that either. But, again, if with bats it will work, why should it not work with humans?" Then he laughed.

"What are you laughing at?" Hi asked.

"The cure," Po said. "Wait till you hear what it is."

Hi patiently waited for Po to stop chortling.

17

Nova Dolencia

BACK IN HI'S RENTED BUNGALOW, McKay looked down at the expanse of the Amazon basin as shown on the map that Hi and Diego unfolded on the kitchen table. To the Britisher it was a disheartening sight.

"Over four million square kilometers," McKay muttered.

"Don't make it sound so bad," Hi said, looking over a particular region. "Try two and a half million square miles."

"How can we hope to find Hitler's camp," McKay asked, "with over four million—"

"Stop worrying, McKay," Hi said irritably. "I know where to find him."

"What?" McKay gasped. "Why didn't you tell me?"

"You didn't ask. I know the general area. That narrows it down."

"What was the clue?" asked Diego.

"Eva's earrings," Hi said. "They were carved out of vilca wood."

Diego snapped his fingers. "Nova Dolencia."

"What," McKay asked them both, "are you talking about?"

Hi pointed it out on the map. "This village, McKay. The only place in the world where they make and sell vilca-wood earrings."

Hi was pointing to a dot on a branch of the Purús River, about three hundred miles southwest of Manaus, in Brazil's Amazonas province. The heart of the *selva* or rain forest.

"Nova Dolencia," Diego repeated. "The Nazis must get their supplies there."

"Right," Hi said, his eyes poring over the area. "There's no other village for a good hundred miles."

"Then the people there should be able to point the way," McKay said eagerly.

"For a price," Hi told McKay. "Be prepared to buy some vilca-wood earrings."

Less than one week later, the three men flew in Diego's single-engine, four-seat Cessna 170 from Peru to Canutama, Brazil. This small *selva* town on the Purús—a river flowing north, from the Andes of Peru, for over two thousand miles, to join the Amazon at Manaus—had the closest airstrip to Nova Dolencia.

Buying an outboard motorboat and enough supplies for a two-week jungle reconnaissance, the trio spent two and a half days going north from Canutama on the meandering Purús.

For McKay, new to the tropical rain forest, the humidity was oppressive and the scenery monotonous. The river was turbid, its low-banked, jungle-lined waters muddy brown from the rain forest's drainage. The constant meanders made a straight-line mile seem eternal. The crocodile-like caimans made McKay nervous at first, but they soon became tiresome, as did the squawking birds and the chattering monkeys. But occasional jaguars were seen, the snakes weren't your garden variety, and a caiman prowls also at night. McKay refused to sleep on the bank, yet got little sleep in the boat, for fear of some night creature's jaws. Even vampires weren't out of the question.

NOVA DOLENCIA

On the third day Hi navigated the boat into a Purús tributary. They headed south on this serpentine branch, walled by unbroken jungle. There was no hint that human beings had ever been there before, till to McKay' surprise, on the fifth day out of Canutama, they passed the vestiges of some kind of estate, its few crumpled ruins long since reclaimed by the jungle. Diego informed McKay that it was once a rubber plantation. Finally, not far downstream from the ruins, Hi, Diego, and McKay reached Nova Dolencia.

The village was a collection of thatch-roofed buildings made of bamboo and wood from Brazil nut trees. Its founders were *caboclos* (Brazilians of mixed white and Indian blood) from drought-ridden northeast Brazil. They had come to Amazonas in 1910 to work on the rubber plantation. But within two years there was no plantation to work on. Due to Malayan competition, Brazil's rubber economy collapsed and never bounced back. Now the villagers got by as best they could, fishing, foraging, and exporting forest products, such as Brazil nuts and rosewood oil, to distant Manaus by canoe. And virtually all were involved in some way in the crafting or selling of vilca-wood earrings.

The earrings were an innovation of the late Euclides Vidigal, one of the village's founders. And when it came to haggling over earrings, McKay proved no match for the local *tendeiro* or shopkeeper, thirty-four-year-old Maneco Vidigal. This slender, bright-eyed, blackbearded son of Euclides was a natural-born haggler. And since customers in Nova Dolencia were about as frequent as snow, Maneco made the most of each opportunity. Though a merchant in Manaus carried the earrings for a while in his shop, they simply lost their mystique there, selling poorly. Nova Dolencia—if for some reason you found yourself there—

was *the* place to buy vilca-wood earrings. And Maneco's store was the spot.

Hi and Diego served McKay well enough as interpreters, but the Portuguese-speaking Maneco, knowing he had something that these fellows wanted (or at least *they* seemed to think so), was in a position to name his own price. His own quantity too. McKay wound up buying three goodsized cardboard boxes full of vilca-wood earrings. Maneco even charged for the boxes. McKay didn't really mind the money—his operational budget, after all, was virtually unlimited—but there was the immediate logistical problem of what to do with some thirty thousand vilca-wood earrings. As the news of this staggering earring sale got around, the denizens of Nova Dolencia exuberantly began planning a celebration that would last fourteen days.

Maneco agreed, as his part of the bargain, to arrange for a "certain party" in Nova Dolencia to meet with McKay, to divulge confidentially what this certain party might know concerning "nonindigenous groups" (to use McKay's term) in the area. The meeting took place as scheduled on the evening of the following day, in the village's restaurant, which was little more than a lamp-lit shack by the river. Hi and Diego again served as interpreters. The certain party turned out to be Maneco himself, though he claimed that the party originally scheduled was indisposed as a result of the first day's celebration.

While thus enjoying a large meal at McKay's further expense, Maneco had information more useful than he himself realized. Every couple of months, he told the three men, a European "military-type" officer and two or three "privates" would come to Nova Dolencia. They came from somewhere west of the river, to buy mostly food, candles, gasoline, and kerosene. They crossed the river by canoe. ("No," the puzzled Maneco replied to a question from Hi, no one had seen them "fly over.") The officer was called something like "house furor," and the privates were something like "shits." They were pale and said little except to complain. They spoke in incomplete Portuguese sentences, with the help of a pocket dictionary full of "lengthy, weird-looking words." Maneco wondered what they were doing in the jungle, but was glad they had come there with money. He gathered they had generators and kerosene lamps. "Yes," he replied to Hi, they had bought some vilca-wood earrings. But only one pair. Maneco vividly recalled the house furor griping about having to buy them for "that bitch from BA," which in Portuguese was not easy to say.

Since Hi, Diego, and McKay knew that vampires had no need for ordinary foodstuffs, they readily concluded that Hitler and his bloodsucking cronies were maintaining captives as their blood source. When Hi wondered aloud what "house furor" meant, McKay said it was probably a Hauptsturmführer, the SS equivalent of captain.

When asked where he thought the "military-types" were located, Maneco related the story of a small group of foragers from the village who had happened across some buildings in a clearing, about five miles northwest from the river. The foragers left in a hurry when an armed shit approached them. It was clearly the place where the house furor and friends, judging by their paleness, stayed holed up during the day.

As the meeting concluded, McKay left a tip for the waiter, a conscientious lad of thirteen, and asked the boy what he owed for the meal. The boy informed him that the restaurant belonged to his father Maneco, who then figured up McKay's bill.

On the following day, while drunken revelry in Nova

Dolencia continued, Hi, Diego, and McKay, wearing camouflage uniforms, set out on reconnaissance northwest from the river. They buried the three boxes of earrings once out of sight of the village. ("I'll be damned," McKay had said bitterly, "if I'll give one pair back to those leeches.") This reduced what they had to carry to food and drink, three guns with ammunition, three machetes, and three sets of hammers and stakes.

The hammers and stakes were precautionary. The purpose of the reconnaissance was to locate, not yet to confront, the undead foe. Any confrontation now and Hi, Diego, and McKay knew they would not make it back to the village. They could not pretend to be innocent jungle explorers, not with Wolfgang's acquaintance with Hi. And even innocent explorers would likely be drained of their blood. No, the best that the three men could hope for, if discovered, would be to take one or two Nazis down with them.

The Nazis, by their periodic visits, were wearing a rudimentary trail through the *selva*, which away from the river did not have much undergrowth under its light-blocking canopy. Hi, Diego, and McKay proceeded to follow the path, winding their way through the rain forest. As Hi led the way, his mind was filled with recurring voices, commenting on the challenge ahead. He heard Eva say, "Don't come after us, Hi. Please." He heard McKay's voice again: "We must save the world from Hitler Part Two." He heard Juan weep and whine, "Kill Hitler, kill them all, but save Evita. Bring her back." He heard Eva say, "I was so sick of Juan."

On the second day out, they found Hitler.

Part Two
Der Führer

1

Rudolf the Blackshirt Loony

Hidden in the thick vegetation that bordered the clearing, Hi, Diego, and McKay looked over the compound. It was their second quick look. After the first they had retreated a few yards back in the undergrowth, till one of four armed Schützes, patrolling the compound's perimeter at evenly spaced intervals, had walked past at the clearing's edge. The four pale Nazis on patrol, Mauser rifles in hand, looked evil enough as Schutzstaffel goons. The fact that they were vampires gave them an extra aura of hellishness. Hi had already tangled with one creep from this place, and wasn't ready yet to deal with a bunch. Hi and his comrades had only a few moments to sneak forward and get the compound in sight again before the next Schütze would pass.

They spoke in whispers as they took in the layout. "Looks pretty quiet," Hi said. "Most of 'em are probably asleep, like good little vampires."

"That balcony with the swastika," McKay said, studying Neuanfang's Gebäude Ein (Building One) through binoculars. "Guess whose quarters."

Diego read the Gothic script on the plaque above the balcony: " 'Neuanfang.' What does that mean?"

" 'New Beginning,' " Hi said.

Diego chuckled. "We'll put a stop to that," he said. Then he looked at Hi. "How do we do it?"

"Let's get back to Nova Dolencia," Hi said, "and figure it out." The next Schütze would soon walk past, and they had seen about all they could see anyway without going onto the premises. They crept back a few yards through the shielding undergrowth, then waited till the Schütze, who still might possibly hear them, had time to go by. They then headed back for Nova Dolencia through the dense foliage, Hi leading the way.

The undergrowth thinned out the deeper they went into the canopied jungle. "I've got to get to Manaus," McKay finally said, walking last behind Diego, "and get word to my superiors. They can have commandos out here in a matter of—"

"That's not the way," Hi interrupted over his shoulder. "We can't simply go in with commandos. Not at first."

"Why not?" McKay wanted to know.

"Because of Eva. I'm bringing her back—alive, so to speak." Hi stopped and waited for McKay, to look the Britisher firmly in the eye. "We're taking no chance of having her killed with the others. Now that we have a cure."

"The cure sounds pretty farfetched to me," McKay groused. He wasn't prepared to argue for killing Hi's used-to-be, whom Hi clearly desired as his will-be-again.

"I'm willing to try it," Hi said. "Got any better ideas?" Hi turned and resumed walking, Diego and McKay following. "What are commandos going to do anyway? Shoot 'em? That won't faze a vampire. Chase 'em with hammers and stakes? Or crosses? Or garlic?"

"And what would *you* do?" McKay countered, almost shouting over Diego's shoulder at Hi. "Have them force-fed with that Chinaman's extract, then wait for six hours?"

"Five hours and a half," Hi said, brushing a long fern stalk out of his way. Diego, following, caught the stalk with his hand.

"Don't get cute with me, Hickenlooper," McKay warned.

"Shut up," Diego told McKay. Diego let go of the stalk and it hit McKay in the face. Diego asked Hi, "Got any kind of plan, compadre?"

"With that guy around?" After a moment Hi said, "I'll have one by this time tomorrow."

Hi spent the next day by the river at Nova Dolencia. He was thinking, scheming, and preferred to do it alone. While Hi sat staring at the river's brown water, Diego and McKay bounced around some ideas of their own, in the shack the three rented from Maneco. As they talked, Diego and McKay cracked Brazil nuts and drank pineapple juice. They had to keep the shack open, to get a little breeze, despite the drunken whoops and ceaseless samba music outside.

McKay favored dropping some atomic bombs, one on the Nazi compound itself and two or three in the surrounding area, to make sure all the vampires were fried. Diego suggested a conventional force, overwhelming the Nazis, whether vampires or not, with sheer numbers. Hitler, after all, was a war criminal, and ought to be put on trial. What a nitwit, thought McKay. He reminded Diego that this was a secret operation. The world would be better off not knowing, after so many lives had been lost, that Hitler not only had given the Allies the slip, but was now potentially immortal. It would be a black eye for Ike, Churchill, and everyone else. No, IQ would quietly handle this matter, while the world went about its business.

Diego asked how atomic explosions—assuming they would have any lasting effect on vampires—could be kept secret. "We would use small bombs," McKay answered. And what, asked Diego, about Nova Dolencia, which might take virtually a direct hit? "That's the beauty of it,"

McKay said, "it would blow this place off the map." And what, Diego asked, about Eva? McKay threw down his Brazil nuts with disgust. "Stop asking questions," he said, "and think up some answers yourself."

That night, in Maneco's shack of a restaurant, Hi was too busy thinking to eat. Maneco's son had served them three bowls of fish soup, prepared with one fish cut in thirds. Hi was served the tail, but ignored it. Diego got the middle and dug in, while McKay, who was given the head, just nibbled around the gills.

"You don't want the eyes?" asked Diego.

"Nah, you can have 'em," McKay said, shoving the whole bowl toward Diego.

"I've got a plan," Hi announced. His companions looked at him eagerly. "It's going to take coordination. I'll be depending on you for the clockwork, McKay. And we'll need some help from my father. I'll leave that up to you, Diego. I'm not going to have time."

"May we have some details?" McKay asked. "What will you be doing?"

Hi smiled. "I'm going to pull a Rudolf Hess."

McKay stared at Hi incredulously. Diego was puzzled. "Who was Rudolf Hess?" Diego asked.

"Hitler's top henchman," McKay said, still staring at Hi. "Until he took it upon himself to parachute into Scotland during the war."

Diego asked, "Why did he parachute into Scotland?"

McKay sighed with impatience. "He was a nut! He thought he could get the British to surrender." McKay looked hard at Hi. "What do you mean you're going to 'pull a Rudolf Hess'?"

Hi shrugged as if the answer was simple. "I'm going to parachute right into their camp."

2
Neu(neu)anfang

BEFORE HI, DIEGO, AND McKAY reembarked for Canutama and the plane, Hi told Maneco that he was not to mention their presence in Nova Dolencia when the "house furor" came around. If Maneco didn't keep his mouth shut, Hi warned him, a team of sociopathic contract criminals would be dispatched by McKay's organization to burn down Nova Dolencia. They would eradicate the vilca-wood earring business in general and Maneco Vidigal in particular. Hi wasn't sure how well he expressed this in Portuguese, but Maneco seemed impressed and agreed to keep quiet.

After the boat trip back to Canutama, the trio flew to Manaus, to establish the necessary communications for the operation. While McKay contacted IQ, Hi sent a telegram to Juan Perón. The items Hi requested arrived by air the next day, along with a tearstained note: "Bring her back to me. Bring back my Evita." That damn Perón. Hi wondered how Juan could explain to his people that Eva was back when her corpse had been displayed to the world. The wimp probably intended to keep Eva hidden in a basement somewhere. But Hi would have to worry about that later.

On the final night in their Manaus hotel, Hi, Diego, and McKay reviewed Hi's plan in minute detail. Though McKay didn't say so, he disliked the plan, because if it worked, Hi would get most of the glory. Diego, sensing this concern of McKay, reminded him, when Hi was not present, that this was a secret operation. There would be no glory involved. That got McKay's goat. He didn't say so, but there would be plenty of glory within the ranks of IQ. "I am pleased to hear," he told Diego sarcastically, "there'll be no tickertape parade in New York."

Thereafter, as Diego would note, McKay always referred to Hi's plan as "our" plan.

They took off the next day in the Cessna, after removing the door from Hi's side of the plane. Hi, who had jumped once before back in college, wore his camouflage suit and a parachute. He had a haversack, and attached to a thin leather strap around his neck was a little cloth bag.

When they spotted the compound, Hi got set as Diego maneuvered the plane for the jump. "Remember, exactly a hundred and twenty days," Hi reminded them.

"Right," McKay said, leaning forward from his seat in back.

"At sunrise."

"See you then," Diego said.

Hi glanced back at the man from IQ. "McKay, I once dreamed of being an intelligence agent. But nothing like this. Much obliged."

McKay smiled and nodded. He decided that this chap was all right, in his own little way.

Hi jumped.

On the compound the Schützes patrolling had heard the distant plane engine, and spotted the plane banking high overhead. One of the Schützes quickly went to find a superior. He came across the Scharführer (sergeant), dozing in some shade. The Schütze could not have found a worse excuse for a superior than this oxy moron. The Scharführer had a thick-lipped mouth that hung open, and eyes that always looked scared, for the Scharführer was always confused. After looking up through binoculars at the open parachute, the Scharführer went to find a superior. He found the sturdy, square-jawed Hauptsturmführer, who looked up and saw Hi in the sky.

"Someone," said the Hauptsturmführer, "is pulling a Rudolf Hess."

"Who was Rudolf Hess?" asked the Scharführer.

The Hauptsturmführer gave him a look, then said, "Awake Obergruppenführer Kegel."

"Are you sure?" asked the Scharführer fearfully.

"Awake him," his superior ordered.

As the Scharführer hustled to Kegel's quarters in Gebäude Ein, Hi looked down with concern at the same building. He was falling toward it. He had hoped for an accurate landing, but this one looked entirely too perfect. "Good start, Hiram," he said to himself. "You're going to land in the Führer's lap."

The Scharführer, reaching Kegel's marble-pocked downstairs quarters, stepped nervously to the open coffin in which uniformed Kegel slept. "Obergruppenführer Kegel," he addressed him, trying not to startle him by being too loud. Kegel still slumbered. After a moment's hesitation, the Scharführer, his mouth hanging more open than usual, gently shook Kegel's arm and spoke louder: "Obergruppenführer."

Kegel's eyes opened. They looked hard at the Scharführer, the rest of Kegel's body not moving. "How dare you disturb me," Kegel said.

The Scharführer quaked in his jackboots. "I was only following orders."

Kegel began getting out of the coffin. "What is wrong?" he asked wearily.

"We are not sure, sir."

"Not sure?"

"Someone is pulling a Rudolf Hess."

Kegel looked at the Scharführer with shock. "Parachuting into the camp? Who would be fool enough to do that?"

Kegel and the Scharführer headed for the entrance hall. This hall, like the building itself, was two stories high. On one wall was a huge enlargement of a photograph of Hitler leaving his Berlin bunker by night. He was smiling and giving the V sign—for Vampire and Victory. Emblazoned beneath Hitler's image was the name he had given the compound: NEUANFANG.

Just as Kegel and the Scharführer hurried into the hall, Hi came crashing through its thatch roof. Kegel and the Scharführer covered their heads as thatch and wood fragments fell on them.

The Hauptsturmführer and a Schütze came hurrying in. The four Nazis looked up at Hi. His parachute had caught on the roof, leaving Hi dangling several feet off the floor. A wooden roof beam with thatch still attached had fallen against the wall photo. It made smiling Hitler look like he was wearing a ridiculous thatch wig.

"Hi Hickenlooper here," Hi announced. Though Hi said it in English, the Nazis thought it was German, the words sounding the same either way.

Kegel pointed at the photo and screamed at the Schütze, "Get that thatch down!" Kegel then put his hands on his hips as he looked up at Hi. "And to what," Kegel asked Hi in German, "do we owe the pleasure of your dropping in?"

Hi smiled cagily and said, "Take me to your leader."

Kegel and the Hauptsturmführer exchanged looks. They took Hi instead, after relieving him of his wallet and little cloth bag, to a small room in Gebäude Drei. They sat

him down on a hard wooden stool, which was the room's only furniture. Even the light-bulb socket hanging over Hi's head was empty, till a Schütze came in with a bulb. Somewhere Hi heard a gasoline-powered generator start, lighting the bulb. They then left Hi alone with it burning,
 After several minutes, Kegel returned with Obergruppenführer Dorsch. Hi, who was pacing, obligingly sat down as they entered.
 "Where do you come from?" Dorsch demanded. "Whose plane brought you here?"
 Hi was happy to explain. "I hired a private pilot to drop me off over the jungle. Don't worry. He knows nothing."
 The Obergruppenführers couldn't figure Hi's accent. "Are you German?" Kegel asked.
 "And proud of it," Hi said. "My mom was from Hamburg. It was Mom who got Dad into hamburgers. My dad's father came from the Rhineland."
 "Which part?" Dorsch asked. "I'm from Mainz."
 "Who cares where you're from?" Kegel snapped.
 Hi saw that Kegel had his little cloth bag. Kegel opened it, and demonstratively poured some plant seeds into one hand.
 "What are these?" Kegel asked.
 "What do they look like?" Hi said. "They're seeds."
 "What *kind* of seeds?" Kegel smiled meanly.
 "Ever heard of the dragon's palm?"
 The two Nazis' expressions told Hi they had not.
 "I was hoping you hadn't," Hi said. "I hope you realize you're tampering with a gift for the Führer. And he's going to be mighty pissed."
 "Who are you?" Dorsch demanded again. "What are you doing here?"
 "I've already told your gift-tampering friend here," Hi said to Dorsch. "The name's Hi Hickenlooper. And I'm here to see the Führer."

Dorsch and Kegel looked at Hi as if they could kill him. But Hi knew that they wouldn't. He had planted seeds of doubt in their minds, infertile though those minds seemed to be. They couldn't afford to lay a hand on—or sink a tooth in—him yet.

3
Bamboozlers

ADOLF HITLER watched as Kegel carefully dumped a few plant seeds from the little cloth bag onto a piece of cloth spread on the Führer's mahogany desk. Hitler was standing behind the desk with arms folded. His vampiric pallor only amplified the demonic visage that had haunted the civilized world. Night had fallen outside. The Führer, despite news of an intruder, had spent all afternoon on his memoirs, then had napped in his coffin till eight. (He had heard something fall through the roof, but Dorsch and Kegel had handled it.) His second-floor quarters were Spartan, but had a pleasant bamboo decor, the base's only mahogany coffin, and a balcony overlooking the compound. The room was well lit with kerosene lamps. It was Kegel, knowing Hitler loved symbols, who had suggested a bamboo motif, Hitler having bamboozled the world. No one pointed out that bamboo is so hollow inside.

Hitler leaned forward to gaze at the seeds, while Kegel and Dorsch stood in front of the desk.

"What kind of seeds are they?" Hitler asked.

"He spoke of a dragon's palm," Kegel said. "He calls this a gift, to be discussed only with you." Kegel handed Hitler a small photo. "Please note, mein Führer, this photograph, found in the intruder's wallet." It was a picture of a Dracaena palm. "It is a plant. Perhaps the palm of which he speaks."

"I have seen that plant somewhere before," Dorsch said, thoughtfully rubbing one of his chins.

Hitler dropped the photo onto the desk. He began musingly pacing. "Who would carry pictures of plants around in his wallet?" he wondered aloud.

"Only a plant would, mein Führer," Dorsch said. Kegel signaled for Dorsch to be quiet.

Hitler continued to muse. "How did he know we are here?"

"That is what we must learn," Dorsch said, glancing defiantly at Kegel.

"I will torture it out of him," Kegel said. His mouth savored the word "torture" like blood.

"Allow me to offer my assistance," Dorsch said with feigned graciousness.

"Very kind of you," noted Kegel, smiling falsely.

Hitler picked up a few seeds between his fingers, for a closer look at them. He smelled them. There was a faint and not very pleasant odor. "Not edible, I assume," Hitler said.

"Would you like me to eat one?" Dorsch offered.

Hitler sprinkled the seeds back onto the cloth. "No," he said. "Not yet anyway." He regarded the seeds for a moment, then looked at Dorsch. "I want you to bring him to me."

For Hi the hours had dragged in the small locked room where he alternately sat and paced. When Dorsch unlocked the door and entered, Hi impatiently rose from his seat. "I demand to see the Führer," Hi said.

"Your demand is accepted."

"It is? Wait. I demand to use a bathroom first."

Dorsch and a Schütze escorted Hi to a bathroom. As Hi urinated, a torrent of thoughts ran through his mind. He tried to go over mentally what to say to the Führer. He wondered if vampires pee red. He also felt bad about locking up Soto for two days with no baño.

When Dorsch took Hi into Hitler's quarters, the Führer was seated comfortably behind the desk in his bamboo swivel chair. Kegel stood smirking nearby. Hitler stared coldly at Hi, who looked thrilled at the sight of the Führer. Hi clicked his heels and gave the Nazi salute. "Heil Hitler!"

Hitler, Dorsch, and Kegel just stared.

"It's an honor to meet you, mein Führer," Hi gushed. "An absolute honor. I've been an admirer of yours since—well, since I read about the Beer Hall Putsch of 1923. I've been an admirer of your officers too. The kind of guys you have around you. That's what I want to be. There's nothing like being a Nazi. Right, guys? Especially the nocturnal kind."

After a moment, Hitler quietly asked him, "How did you know we were here?"

Hi promptly pulled a chair up to the front of the desk. "Well you see, mein Führer—" Hi then remembered his manners. "May I sit down?" he asked politely.

When he got no response, Hi sat down.

"You see, mein Führer, I have the reputation—I assume they told you my name, it's Hickenlooper. Hi."

"Hi," Hitler said. He didn't know if it was a name or a greeting.

"I have the reputation—well earned, I might add—of knowing the Amazon jungle better than any other fellow alive. So well, in fact, that IQ—the Intelligence Quorum—wanted me to help find you. Well I've found you, but not to help them. I'm here on my own. They don't even know where I am."

Hitler continued to stare.

"You can imagine my excitement," Hi went on, "when IQ told me the story—you being alive, a vampire here in the jungle."

"And why are you here?" Hitler asked.

Hi looked surprised by the question, as if the answer were obvious. "I want to be a part of it," he said. "I want to be a part of your team."

Hitler stared for a moment longer. Then his eyes, as Hi noted, moved to the seeds and photo on his desk.

"I know a bag of seeds, mein Führer, may not look like much of a gift," Hi said. "But it's a token of my sincerity." Eager to explain, Hi pulled his chair closer to the desk. "These are seeds, mein Führer, of the Dracaena palm. Dracaena means dragon. The picture is of the plant full grown. The ancient Greeks named this plant in honor of vampires. It makes a great house plant."

"My God," Dorsch interjected, suddenly remembering. "He is right, mein Führer. The castle of the Countess. That is where I saw that plant."

"Who's the Countess?" Hi asked.

"The Countess," Dorsch said, "is a lady who—"

"It's none of his business who the Countess is!" Kegel angrily told Dorsch.

After a moment Hi continued. "I know you like symbols, mein Führer—the swastika and all. I thought you might like to spruce up the place with some plants virtually named in your honor."

Hitler rose from his chair and began thoughtfully pacing. Hi waited, then said rather sheepishly, "I'm sorry if you don't like the plant, mein Führer. I could have brought a cake, but I was afraid it might get squashed when I landed."

"So you want to be a part of my team," Hitler said, still pacing.

"Yes, mein Führer," Hi said, rising expectantly from his chair.

"You want to be a vampire."

"Very much so. I'd be eternally grateful."

Hitler stopped pacing and regarded Hi. "And what have you to offer? Besides a bag of seeds."

"Knowledge, mein Führer," Hi said. "To begin with, I am fluent in German."

"So what?" Kegel said. "How's your Portuguese?"

"Fluent there too," Hi exaggerated. "And there's my unrivaled knowledge of this jungle, mein Führer, which serves as your refuge. I can serve as your eyes, your ears, as the need may arise."

Hitler thought that a good point. But it was the next point that really impressed him. "And a fortune," Hi said. "I am the sole heir of Hickenlooper Foods, one of the largest food companies in America. Every penny shall be at your disposal, as soon as my father is gone." Hitler began pacing again, somewhat faster than before. "All I ask in return, mein Führer, is the opportunity to serve you. Forever."

Hitler stopped, looked again at Hi, then glanced toward the Obergruppenführers. "What do you think, Herr Dorsch? Herr Kegel?"

"This food-giant father of yours," Kegel said to Hi. "How well is he?"

"He's got a bad heart," Hi lied. "He could go any day."

Hitler looked at Dorsch for his thoughts. "There is much food for thought here," Dorsch said.

"May I suggest," Kegel said, "a trial period for Herr Hickenlooper. Probationary status."

"Subject, of course, to immediate termination," Dorsch added.

"Such as a dip in our pool," Kegel said.

Hitler was letting these dolts feel important. He had already made his decision. In addition to the points made, the Führer had thought of something else—something vitally important, and having nothing to do with the jungle, a fortune, or plants—that made this fellow seem almost a godsend.

"You are accepted, Herr Hickenlooper," Hitler said, walking back to his desk chair, "on a provisional basis."

"Thank you, mein Führer," Hi exulted.

"Your knowledge, not to mention your fortune, may indeed come in handy." Hitler sat down.

"What a moment," Hi said. "My mom would be some kind of proud. I can't tell you how much this means, I—"

"Then don't," Kegel stopped him. "You have taken enough of the Führer's time." Kegel signaled to Dorsch to take Hi away.

Hi looked at the seeds, which were still on Hitler's desk. Hi of course wanted to be in charge of the plant's cultivation—and he wanted to get on with it. But he didn't want to make an issue of it, seeming pushy, right then, lest he arouse suspicion just when he had them bamboozled. Hi would wait. He saluted Hitler again with a raised arm and click of the heels. Hitler, his eyes having returned to his memoirs, half-raised an acknowledging hand. Hi turned to leave, Dorsch set to follow him.

"I do like the plant," Hitler said. Hi stopped and turned at the door. Hitler had picked up the photo and was regarding it. "It will add just the right touch." The Führer suddenly became angry. "Why did no one tell me before of this palm of the dragon's existence?"

For a moment Dorsch and Kegel didn't know what to say. "Why didn't you tell him?" Kegel then asked Dorsch accusingly.

"Because," Dorsch blustered, "because I thought that *you* would."

Hi acted puzzled as he returned from the door. "But

you didn't know," he told Dorsch. "When I asked you, you—"

"I *did* know," Dorsch insisted.

"So did I," Kegel said.

"No," Hitler said, thinking back. "No, Dorsch, you couldn't even remember where—"

"Take him out," Kegel evasively told Dorsch with a nod toward Hi.

"Neither one of you knew," Hitler said.

"I am taking him out," Dorsch evasively told Kegel.

"You showed me this photo," said Hitler, "and—"

"You know where to take him," Kegel told Dorsch.

"You said, 'It's some kind of plant,' " Hitler recalled, "and—"

"You come with me," Dorsch told Hi.

"Wait!" Hitler screamed.

Dorsch and Kegel snapped to attention with simultaneous clicks of their heels.

Hitler sighed. "Do you see," he asked Hi, "what I have to deal with?" Then he bellowed at Dorsch, "I'll tell you when to take the man out!"

"I thought, sir," Dorsch said softly, "that Herr Hickenlooper's visit was over."

"It was not," Hitler softly replied. Then he looked kindly at Hi. "You are in charge of the plant's cultivation."

"Thank you, mein Führer," Hi said happily. He wouldn't have to ask after all.

Hitler looked again at Dorsch. "See that he has his own room in Gebäude Zwei," Hitler said in his routinely gruff manner, "and a table to work on."

"I will, mein Führer," Dorsch said. "Is that all?"

Hitler looked at Kegel, who was staring at Hi with resentment. "Don't just stand there, Kegel!" Hitler yelled, Kegel jumping. "Give our new Schütze his seeds!"

4

The Ceremony

DORSCH WAS SULLEN as he escorted Hi down the stairs from Hitler's quarters. The first-floor passage was dark, its plain pine walls and floor visible only in intermittent patches of light provided by wall lamps. The shadows and lamplight made Dorsch's already grotesque profile an eery sight as Hi, who had his haversack and cloth bag of seeds, asked his escort where they were going.

"To your initiation," Dorsch said ominously. Then he added with a cryptic smile, "You are going to have a fun evening." As he looked at Hi, Dorsch noticed something odd, something he couldn't put his finger on, about the way Hi was walking. He had noticed it earlier too. "Do you have a clubfoot?"

"Nah," Hi smiled, "just a spring in my gait." Hi didn't want to be summarily disqualified—and get a dip in the pool, whatever that meant—by the same deformity that had kept him from trying to get Hitler in Europe.

As Hi and Dorsch spoke, Hi paid little attention to the husky Untersturmführer (second lieutenant), walking in the opposite direction, who passed them in the shadows. But though Hi failed to recognize the black-shirted oaf, Wolfgang certainly recognized Hi. Wolfgang wondered what Eva's old flame, of all mortal creatures, was doing in Hitler's lair. Wolfgang knew that he had better find out.

Dorsch first took Hi back to the Gebäude Drei

bathroom, where Hi washed up and changed clothes, putting on a light shirt and slacks from his haversack, into which he put the seeds.

Returning to Gebäude Ein, they proceeded through dark corridors till Dorsch stopped at a closed door and knocked. Before Hi had time to wonder who might respond, Dorsch opened the door. Hi followed Dorsch into a chamber as dimly lit as the corridor. But the soft light here came from candles, which with scarlet drapes, some nice bamboo furniture, a well-pillowed bed, and a large oil painting on the wall, gave the quarters—were it not for an open, empty coffin—a sparsely romantic air.

Then Hi saw that he and Dorsch were not alone. Near a dark, far window, lounging on a loveseat, was the apparently nightgowned form of a woman, her features obscured beyond the flickering light. Staring, Hi was not even aware of Dorsch's departure till the door closed behind him.

The woman rose languidly and walked toward Hi. As the candlelight illumined her features, Hi knew that he had seen her before. In a picture.

"I am Countess Borca," she said, her eyes gazing up into Hi's. She spoke softly, in German, but with little expression. "I am in charge of all initiations."

I'll be damned, Hi thought, at least they're going to make this pleasant. But then he thought, Hell, how can I do this? Countess Borca had been taken from her homeland against her will, and was surely not now laying vampire initiates in the Amazon jungle by choice. Hi almost dared at that moment to take her into his confidence. But he couldn't, not yet. He might, after all, be wrong about her. And for all he knew they were being watched. He had better make this look good.

"Initiate me," Hi said with a smile.

Did she ever. In her arms that night Hi almost forgot why they had brought him to the Countess's quarters. In some other time and place, with no knowledge of who she was, Hi could take her for just what she seemed, an attractive, love-hungry woman, one who knew how to make a man hungry. Hi felt guilty making love to her, but hoped to make it up to her later, to restore her, if all went well, to her faraway castle. Meanwhile, with Hi, at least, she seemed to enjoy her task. But Hi held off orgasm as long as he could, because he knew what would come after he did.

When it came, though, the Countess was gentle. Hi hardly felt the teeth go in, and felt more psychologically than physically the blood being sucked from his neck, until he was no longer conscious of anything.

5

Jackboots and Dagger

HI REGAINED CONSCIOUSNESS, alone on the bed, after an hour or so. There were dried drops of blood on the sheet. He saw the Countess, again in her nightgown, staring thoughtfully into space on the loveseat. Outside was the first light of dawn.

Hi got up, put on his boxer shorts, picked up his undershirt, and went into the Countess's small bathroom. On the cabinet over the sink was a mirror. Hi was afraid to look in it. Come to think of it, he thought, what's a mirror doing here anyway? He finally looked, and found his usual reflection. But his eyes avoided the neck. Hi had done what he had to that night, but the reality still had to sink in. After a moment, he reluctantly stepped closer, and examined the small, clean holes that the Countess's canine teeth had left in his neck.

Hi wondered when and if the bite would take full effect. Loss of blood, he reasoned, should make him feel weak, yet a vampire's strength should offset that. He looked closely at his teeth in the mirror, and saw no change in his canines. But then the Countess's canines also looked normal when she and Hi had first begun making love. Vampires' canines, Hi guessed, only elongate when needed for entry.

The bite then took full effect right before Hi's eyes. He found himself looking at the blank wall behind him. His reflection in the mirror had suddenly disappeared. So *that's* why there's a mirror, Hi thought. Good show.

The Countess was taking something out of a closet as Hi, donning a smile and his undershirt, came out of the bathroom.

"Well, I guess that's it," Hi said with an ambivalent sense of accomplishment. "I'm a vampire."

"How do you feel?"

"Kind of sleepy." Hi felt of his teeth with his tongue. "And I've got this tingling in my teeth."

"That is good." The Countess had taken an SS outfit—black shirt and breeches—from the closet. Hi was about to put on his shirt from the night before.

"No," she said quietly, going to him. She took Hi's shirt and tossed it onto a chair. "Now you wear the black shirt of the Schutzstaffel." She helped Hi on with it.

Hi could see that her heart wasn't in this. As he began buttoning the shirt, she gestured toward the breeches, draped over the back of the chair. "Here are the breeches. Your SS dagger and boots are in the closet."

The Countess went to the loveseat, sat down, and became pensive again as Hi finished dressing. The Countess, given her captivity, tried to take things philosophically. It's how one kept one's sanity. Blood was blood, and fresh blood was better than bottled, which was her usual fare nowadays. Nor was she ever required to have sex, with Hitler or with anyone else. Hi had been a rare treat, she was hungry and wanted him, and Hi thought that he was obliged. But Hitler, Kegel, and the rest of those creeps had been unpleasant meals. Oh, they made a pretense, at least in Berlin, of treating her like royalty. But it was royalty held hostage, in secret, and without any ransom.

"What happens now?" Hi asked, fully uniformed, as he adjusted the sheath of his dagger.

"They will come for you," she said, rising. She walked to the window and began sadly gazing out.

Hi walked over to her side. "Countess Borca, do you ever dream of going home to Romania?"

She turned and looked at him with surprise. Had he been reading her thoughts? She was also suspicious, and said nothing.

"Maybe I can help you get back," Hi said.

"Why do you say this?" she asked. "Who are you?"

"Hi Hickenlooper, German American. You can trust me." Her eyes were searching his. "Would you like to go home?"

"Of course," she said anxiously. "What do you think I am here but a prisoner?"

"Do you ever get out? Why not just fly away?"

"In which direction? Where are we?" She was not aware that a village lay but five miles away. But then the knowledge would have done her no good. "They mock me." She gestured toward the corridor. "There is a rear door to this building, only a few feet away. It is like they are saying, 'A hostage? No, you can walk right out.' But to where? In the daytime no vampire can fly. How far would I get on foot? And at night Schützes take to the air, on patrol." Her voice trembled with anger. "Do you see? They are *daring* me to try to escape. One has told me straight out, that Kegel. He said, 'If *we* can't escape, you can't either. Try it. If we catch you, the stake!'"

There were tears in her eyes. Hi took her hand. "I'm your ticket to Romania," he whispered assuringly. "I'm here to get Hitler. And every Schutzstaffel dog in this jungle. Are you with me?"

"Yes," she said without hesitation.

They heard Dorsch loudly greet someone as he came to the closed door of the chamber.

"Where can I find Eva Perón?" Hi quickly asked the Countess.

Dorsch knocked on the door. "Herr Hickenlooper!" he called.

"Down the hall," the Countess said hurriedly, "first door on the right."

Dorsch opened the door and walked in. Stopping, he stood there and smirked at Hi and the Countess.

"Good morning," Hi said. Dorsch said nothing, just smirked, as Hi put his clothes in the haversack. Hi then looked at the Countess. "Thanks for the initiation."

"You are welcome," she said, meaning it.

Hi went into the corridor and waited for Dorsch, who stood smiling at the Countess. Dorsch was remembering his own initiation of sorts. It was only a long bite in Berlin, but he still felt those lips on his neck. But then Dorsch, as he found out at Castle Borca, could be sexually aroused by a faceful of shit. For her part, Countess Borca found Dorsch's lascivious smile not only nauseating but insubordinate. Hitler had it understood that no one, once initiated, was to bother the Countess again. Before turning away, she bared her teeth at Dorsch with mocking contempt.

Dorsch sulked as he escorted Hi to Gebäude Zwei. Hi noticed, walking between the buildings, that the early morning sun felt unusually hot on his skin. In Gebäude Zwei, most of the Nazis below Frankel's rank, including some thirty Schützes, were turning in for the day. As Dorsch and Hi walked down the first-floor corridor, Dorsch pointed out the floor's communal bathroom. From their doorways along either side of the corridor, pale, mean-looking Schützes regarded Hi with curiosity, and were resentful that he got his own room. Before Hi only the Oberschützes and other officers below the rank of Sturmbannführer had private rooms in Gebäude Zwei. (Kegel, Dorsch, Müller, and Frankel had quarters in Gebäude Ein.) Hi's room wasn't much, though, to envy, any more than the others. It contained a pair of cheap coffins, an old bamboo chair, a chipped wooden stool, and bare Paraná pine walls.

Dorsch and Hi stepped to one of the coffins. Hi opened it, felt the loose padding, tossed in his haversack, then looked the room over.

"Very nice," Hi told Dorsch. "I like Early Cave."

Dorsch, turning to leave, said, "Have a good day's sleep."

"Thanks. What time do we eat? I mean drink."

"The blood flows at midnight."

"Sounds good." Hi was surprised to hear himself say that so matter-of-factly.

"It flows down the hallway," Dorsch said.

"The blood 'flows down the hallway'?"

"The *drink hall*," Dorsch explained, pointing, "is *there*, down the hallway."

Hi looked around again as Dorsch turned to leave. "Obergruppenführer." Dorsch stopped at the door and looked back. "Where's my table?"

Dorsch glared at Hi, then walked over to him and got right in Hi's face. In a hissing, hate-filled whisper, Dorsch said, "You will get your table, Herr Hickenlooper. But do not forget one thing: you are a Schütze. A lowly, insignificant Schütze."

Hi didn't bat an eye. He loved being hated by Dorsch. As Dorsch again turned and walked toward the door, Hi said, "Lowly, yes. Insignificant, no."

Dorsch again stopped and looked back at him. Hi smiled with self-satisfaction.

"I think Hitler likes me," Hi said.

6

Der Untersturmführer

Hi had to see Eva, and let her know he was there. If someone else told her first, in her surprise she could ruin everything by saying or doing something wrong. She had to be prepared, and to pretend not to know him. He had to pray she had not, at some point, already innocently mentioned her former lover to Hitler, and if she had, that it wasn't by name. As best Hi could tell in their meeting, Hitler had never heard of Hi Hickenlooper. Hi had considered, of course, coming in under an assumed name. But that would have been foolish, since Wolfgang could easily expose the lie. No, Hi had to be seemingly as genuine as his mission allowed—he was already a *vampire*, wasn't he?—and play the Wolfgang angle by ear.

Wolfgang. He remained the big fly in the ointment.

Hi would wait till he thought it was safe, all the Nazis on Gebäude Zwei's first floor tucked in their coffins. He planned, as he waited, how to reach Eva's quarters. He assumed that Gebäude Ein, housing Hitler, Eva, and the Schutzstaffel brass, was off limits except for official business, which, again Hi assumed, was conducted at night. He had seen two Schützes standing guard—actually one was sitting at a picnic table and quickly got up—in front of Gebäude Ein when Dorsch brought him out through the double-door entrance that morning. But Gebäude Ein, as the Countess had incidentally informed him, had a rear door, only a few feet from her quarters. When leaving that morning, Hi saw that it was latched from inside. And while Dorsch lingered in the Countess's chamber, Hi, who knew he had to get back in the building to Eva, had had the presence of mind to step quickly over and unlatch the rear door.

Hi had waited long enough. He stole down the Gebäude Zwei corridor to the drink hall, which contained plain wooden tables and benches. From there he could exit the building, through a door facing the jungle, its foliage only a few yards away. Peeking out the door, Hi waited till one of the Schützes on patrol had walked past, then he hurried out on tiptoe to enter the tangled vegetation. Hi made his way laboriously, as quietly as possible, through the thick undergrowth surrounding the compound, till he had circled around to within several yards of Gebäude Ein's rear door. After again waiting for a Schütze to pass, Hi left the cover of the vegetation and hurried to the door. It was still unlocked, he slipped in. Then he went, as the Countess had directed, to the first door on the right. He quietly opened it and entered.

Eva's quarters, like the Countess's, were a pleasant little oasis among the compound's stark chambers. There were drapes, some mahogany and rosewood furnishings, and bamboo mats. But none of that got Hi's attention. He walked straight to the open coffin, and looked down at sleeping Eva, in a white nightgown. It was eery to see her this way, so similar to the fake Eva lying dead back in Buenos Aires. But this Eva, at least, was undead. Reaching into the coffin, Hi took her upper body gently in his arms, and she awoke as he raised her into a sitting position.

"Hi!" she breathed with surprise, delight, and alarm all at once.

Hi softly kissed her lips as he held her. "Hello, Eva. I'm

going to get you out of this place." Eva looked at him questioningly, at his eyes, his complexion, as she put a loving hand to his face. "Yeah, I'm a vampire," he smiled. "I hope you don't mind that I slept with the Countess last night."

"You mean you made love?"

"Isn't that part of the initiation?"

"She is only required to bite."

Hi couldn't believe it. "You mean I've been raped?" He then wondered about Eva's own initiation into vampirism. "Did you sleep with her too?"

"I slept with Hitler. Sad to say." It then hit her, how much danger Hi was in, and that he had actually joined the undead. "Oh, Hi, how could you—"

"Don't worry," he said soothingly. "I'm counting on a cure. For both of us, once we get out of here."

"A cure?"

"Yeah. Wait till you hear what it is."

"Tell me. Please."

Suddenly someone knocked on the door. The knocks seemed urgent but were not too loud, so as not to awake others.

Eva pointed Hi anxiously to a closet. He quickly entered it, leaving the door slightly cracked open, while Eva got out of the coffin. The door opened and the caller walked in, not waiting for Eva to respond.

It was Wolfgang, in his Untersturmführer garb. "Ah, you are up, Señora." He smiled as she regarded him warily.

"What do you want?" she asked.

"I must speak with you."

"Then come back at a decent hour."

Staying, Wolfgang closed the door. "I must speak with you now." He stepped toward her, Eva took a step back.

"Who do you think you are," she said, "barging in like this?"

They stood looking at each other. "As always, I am a man with your interests in mind."

"What are you talking about?"

Wolfgang took another step forward. "You will never guess, Señora, who I saw last night, being escorted to the Countess."

Eva stood her ground. "I'm sure I could never guess."

"Hi Hickenlooper—the friend in Buenos Aires whom you had me fetch for you."

"Really?" There was no interest at all in her tone.

"Why has he come here?" He stepped closer. "Only for love would someone take such a risk."

Eva tried to turn away. Wolfgang grabbed her arm and pulled her to him. He was smirking.

"It is my duty, Señora, to have the Führer informed." He slipped an arm around her waist. "I could be persuaded, however, to keep your acquaintance confidential."

Wolfgang tried to kiss her. Eva kneed him in the groin as hard as she could. He let go, she stepped back and glared at him, as he grunted, bending slightly in pain. She had enjoyed doing that even more than when she did it to Cuco Rivera.

Hi, continuing to restrain himself behind the closet's cracked-open door, shook a fist as a silent hurrah.

"Swine," Eva snarled at Wolfgang. "How dare you come into my quarters, in the dead of day, thinking I would yield to such blackmail."

"But you will yield, Señora." Wolfgang was mad now, and grabbed her again. "Would you dare to scream for help?" Eva tried to fight him off as he held her. "Could you deny what I would then tell the Führer?" He held her tighter as she struggled in vain. "You must think of your friend if not of yourself."

Wolfgang suddenly felt someone grab his arm, turning

him around with a vampire's daytime strength, Eva slipping out of his arms. Hi's fist smashed straight into Wolfgang's nose. Blood poured onto the oaf's black shirt as he staggered backward to the wall.

Wiping blood from his nose with a sleeve, Wolfgang glared at Hi, who stood waiting for Wolfgang to counter.

"It's a fair fight now, Wolfie," Hi said.

"Hickenlooper." Wolfgang drew his SS dagger from its sheath. "Did you know," he said, smiling through blood as he brandished the weapon, "that a Schutzstaffel dagger in the heart is as good as any stake?"

"Yeah?" Hi drew his dagger. "Vampires shouldn't walk around with 'em. They might trip."

Wolfgang moved toward Hi. "They are needed. For vampires like you."

Wolfgang lunged with his dagger. Hi, deftly dodging the blade, plunged his dagger into Wolfgang's side. Hi's dagger came out as Wolfgang pulled back.

Wolfgang looked down at his bleeding but harmless wound, then back up, with fiery hatred in his eyes, at Hi. Wolfgang lunged again, but Hi was the faster and more agile of the two. Wolfgang's swipe with the dagger missed, but his bulk knocked Hi down, causing Hi's blade, aimed at the heart, to go awry, cutting a slice through Wolfgang's other side.

Standing over Hi, still on the floor with his dagger, the twice-wounded, bleeding Wolfgang was set to attack, when Eva desperately grabbed him from behind. Wolfgang threw her off. Then, going quickly to one knee, the Nazi came down with his dagger toward Hi—but Hi's dagger came up to meet him. It plunged straight into Wolfgang's heart, where Hi left it.

Struggling to his feet, Wolfgang staggered, Hi's dagger buried to the hilt in his blood-pouring chest. He dropped his own dagger, and his hand moved feebly upward as if to try to remove Hi's. But the hand never got there. Hi rolled out of the way as bleeding Wolfgang fell to the floor.

"So long, Wolfie," Hi said, sitting up on the floor beside him. "It's been a real displeasure."

But Wolfgang was now as big a problem as ever. The oaf's blood was all over Eva's floor, and on Hi's uniform too. What was Hi doing in Señora Perón's quarters?

As he and Eva watched Wolfgang die, Hi wondered desperately what to do next.

7

Period of Adjustment

EVA, EMOTIONALLY SPENT, held her forehead, her elbow propped on a rosewood cabinet top. Hi got up from the floor and looked down at dead Wolfgang.
"It took all I could do," Eva said, "not to scream."
Hi looked at her. Scream, he realized, was exactly what she should do. "Scream," he told her. She looked at him quizzically. "Scream as loud as you can."
Eva took a deep breath and screamed. "That's good," Hi said. "But louder."
Eva screamed more and louder. It was enough to wake the undead, and one by one they began arriving, aroused with alarm from their coffins. Kegel came first, and then Dorsch, who came holding his head in pain. Trying to get out of his coffin too hurriedly, Dorsch had tipped it over and landed on his forehead. Then in came Hitler, with the armed Schütze who guarded his upstairs quarters.
No one said a word before Hitler's arrival. Kegel and Dorsch, as usual, had been sleeping in uniform. Hitler wore a black silk robe over white pajamas. Looking first down at Wolfgang, Hitler strode over to Eva, still recovering emotionally by the cabinet.
"I'm all right," she said whisperingly.
Hitler turned to Hi. "What has happened here?"
"I heard this lady scream," Hi said nervously, "and rushed right in. She was being attacked by this, uh—"

"Untersturmführer," Kegel said.

"Whatever. He came at me with his dagger."

Hitler looked at Eva. "This is true?"

"Yes," Eva said. She gestured toward Hi. "This man fought so bravely."

Hitler barely glanced at Hi. Looking down at the bloodsoaked corpse, Hitler began trembling with rage. "This despicable vermin," he said, shaking a finger toward dead Wolfgang, "is the same Untersturmführer who was assigned to protect you." Hitler turned to Eva and screamed, "Do you see, you Argentine firecracker, what happens when you go galavanting outside of this jungle?" Eva remained calm as he ranted. "This Untersturmführer had the uncontrollable hots!"

"So I have a new protector," Eva said quietly, with a glance toward Hi. "Who is he?"

Hitler was starting to calm down. He looked at Hi, then walked over to him. "Herr Hickenlooper," he said. Crossing his arms on his chest, Hitler looked Hi in the eye. Hi found that demonic gaze, at such close range, unsettling. Hitler asked him the question Hi had feared: "What were you doing in Gebäude Ein?"

"Yes," Kegel said, stepping close to Hitler's shoulder and looking Hi in the eye. "What is your explanation?"

Dorsch stepped close to Hitler's other shoulder, and looked Hi in the eye. "What were you doing in Gebäude Ein?"

Hitler looked at the two Obergruppenführers crowding his shoulders. "Dorsch," he said calmly, "go get some Schützes to clean up this mess."

Dorsch started to go, then asked, "Shall we save all the blood, sir?" Hitler gave him a disagreeable look and Dorsch left.

Hitler returned his attention to Hi.

"You were saying?" smiling Kegel said to Hi.

Hi looked almost ashamed. "To tell you the truth," he said reluctantly, "I was coming to see the Countess." Kegel looked at Hitler, who arched an eyebrow at Hi. Kegel did likewise. "But it's not what you think. I need her advice or something. I'm afraid that last night . . . well, it may not have taken."

Hitler's hard look became questioning. "You are still not a vampire?"

"What makes you think that?" Kegel asked.

Hi seemed disgusted with himself. "I've got this craving," he complained, "for a big plate of sauerkraut and a stein of cold beer."

Hitler and Kegel glanced at each other. They looked at Hi and nodded understandingly. "You had better see the Countess," Kegel said.

"I didn't want to tell you," Hi said remorsefully to Hitler. "I don't want to disappoint you. I—"

"Don't worry," Hitler said. He was pleased. It was refreshing to have an intelligent sycophant from outside the old guard. One with obvious mettle. And he still had a use for this Schütze. "Remember," Hitler assured him, "there can be a period of adjustment. Check with the Countess. But I'm sure there's no problem. And tonight you will dine in my quarters."

"Thank you, mein Führer," Hi said.

"We must show you our appreciation," Hitler said, gesturing toward the corpse, "for dispatching this . . . " No sufficient word seemed to come.

"We are very disappointed, mein Führer," Kegel said apologetically, "in the late Untersturmführer."

8

Dinner with Adolf

HITLER'S DINING ROOM, softly lit by kerosene lamps, had bamboo-mat walls and a large mahogany table, in the center of which sat a large punch bowl for each evening meal. On his first full evening as a vampire, Hi was treated at this table as an honored guest—having first gone as instructed to see the Countess, who gave him (after they had a good laugh) a clean bill of health. Their evening together, she assured him, had been a roaring success, and Hi told her that he couldn't agree more.

At the table, in addition to Hitler and Hi, were the Führer's usual dining companions: Eva, Dorsch, Kegel, Müller, and Frankel. Dorsch and Kegel were not pleased with Hi's presence, but since this uppity Schütze was presumably there for one evening, they made the best of it. They didn't faze Hi, but the taciturn Müller made him uncomfortable. Müller seemed intelligent, and suspicion toward Hi, verbally unexpressed, was palpable in his eyes. The personable Frankel found Hi interesting, and joined Hitler in asking the explorer many questions about the Amazon rain forest—a subject that bored Dorsch and Kegel to tears. Eva said little, her eyes seldom leaving Hi. She loved him more than ever for what he was trying to do, for what he had already done, at such incredible risk to himself.

The meal of course consisted of blood, fresh from the

Weinkellar fridge, and was ladled from the punch bowl into glasses by Oberschütze Spitz, a boyish Weinberg aide who doubled as Hitler's waiter. And if Hi had actually had any doubt about being a vampire, it would have been dispelled on this night. The elixir, Hi found, went down perfectly well and was quite satisfying. But that was to be expected. What Hi had to guard against, given such a drastic change in culinary taste, was any similar sea change in attitude.

After the meal, Hi was surprised to be invited to join Hitler alone for a chat on the balcony. This being a special night for the Schütze, Hitler had decided to go ahead and tell him what he specially desired of him. For the first few moments, as they sat in cushioned bamboo chairs and contemplated a full clear moon over the blackness of the jungle around them, the Führer said nothing. Then he launched into a fatuous spiel about being misunderstood and falsely maligned by the world. The truth, he said, was all in his memoirs, which he was laboring to complete. But he was desperate to have someone intelligent, well educated, and reasonably objective—meaning, Hi gathered, not abjectly servile—to critique and help edit them. When Hi asked how much he had written, Hitler told him that so far the first-draft chapters, all written in longhand, took up about one third of Gebäude Drei.

"Well," Hi said, "I can see that you need an editor."

"I would like you to try your hand," Hitler said. "There is no one else I can trust with the task. Dorsch? Kegel? Why, they wouldn't even tell me if I misspelled a word."

"How would they know?"

"Müller? We would get into arguments. What's the point? I would win."

"May I ask you something, mein Führer?"

"Of course."

"Where did you get these guys?"

Hitler stared at Hi for a moment. Hi feared that he had overstepped his bounds. But Hitler took no offense. He had asked the same question himself. "One has to start somewhere," Hitler said. Then he sighed. "But it's hard. As you see, I have had to make do with the dregs, the absolute dregs, of the Schutzstaffel."

"What else did the Schutzstaffel have?" The question was asked without thinking. Hi then had to think fast. "I mean, where *are* they? Where are all the *good men* you had?"

Hitler's brief frown disappeared with Hi's clarification. Hitler leaned his head back on his chair's high back and gazed at the Amazon moon. "All the good ones were lost in the war," he said sadly. "Or got hung after it. Or are somewhere in Paraguay partying." Hitler angrily jerked his head forward. "The ingrates! Now let them come crawling, begging to join Neuanfang. Too late!"

"That's the spirit, mein Führer."

Hitler looked fondly at Hi. "The strength of the thousand-year Reich will lie with new blood, so to speak. Like yourself."

"I don't know what to say." There was a perfect little catch in Hi's voice.

Hitler rose from his chair. "We have much to offer, eh, Schütze? To those who would join us."

"Indeed, sir," Hi said, rising too.

"Immortality is a hard thing to pass up."

"Some people can't live without it."

Hi thought that was funny, but it seemed to be lost on the Führer.

9

Der Oberschütze

THIRTY EVENINGS after dining with Hitler, Hi carried a boxful of one-month-old potted Dracaena palm seedlings into the Führer's lamp-lit quarters. Hitler, writing furiously with a pencil at his desk, was to get the first seedling. Kegel, who escorted Hi in, silently pointed him, so as not to disturb the Führer, to a mahogany work table, which held stacks of Hitler's maniacal scribblings.

Hi set down the box and, after Kegel cleared a central spot by shifting stacks of paper, set the healthiest-looking seedling on the table. Hitler, taking note of Hi, decided to break from his writing. He had been explaining the German defeat in Russia. It had only been a ruse, he tortuously argued, to make the Allies overconfident.

"Good evening, mein Führer," Hi said as Hitler stepped to his side at the table, Kegel centering the Dracaena just right.

"How goes the reading?" Hitler asked. In addition to tending his seedlings, Hi had spent part of each evening, over the last thirty nights, poring over the reams of pure garbage in Gebäude Drei.

"To tell you the truth," Hi said, "I didn't think anyone could top *Mein Kampf*. But so far you've done it."

"That good?"

"We just have to whittle it down. You do tend to go on."

Hi had made Hitler's night. "There's plenty of time for

your editing. We can't publish, after all, till I'm pretty well ruling the world."

"Will that be soon, sir?" Kegel asked delicately. Hitler looked at him. "I mean, you don't have to finish the *writing* first, do you?"

"I'll be finished before you can say Götterdämmerung," Hitler said brusquely. He then regarded the seedling. "It doesn't look like much of a plant."

"It's only a seedling," Hi said. "Give it time. In another, oh, ninety days, you're going to see some kind of change."

Hitler smiled at Hi. Though Hi had stood by the Führer before, being this close to him still gave Hi the creeps. "You are a confident fellow," Hitler said. "You see a plant, you know what you want to get out of it."

"I certainly do."

"I like that, Hickenlooper. You are being promoted." Kegel rolled his eyes.

"Already?" Hi exclaimed.

"From Schütze to Oberschütze." Hitler gave Hi a slap on the shoulder. "Keep up the good work." He headed back to his desk.

"Thank you, mein Führer."

"Get your box," Kegel snarled.

Kegel didn't say another word till he and Hi were outside of the building. In the moonlight they saw Dorsch walking toward Gebäude Vier.

"Obergruppenführer!" Kegel called. Dorsch walked over to meet them between the buildings. "Take this . . . *Ober*schütze—"

Dorsch looked incredulous. "Oberschütze?"

"In another month," Kegel said bitterly, "we'll be calling him Obergruppenführer." Hi, standing there with his seedlings, just smiled. "Take him by the Weinberg and Munitions, will you, to set up his plants."

Dorsch motioned to Hi, who started walking ahead toward Gebäude Vier. Dorsch shook his head as he watched him, then started to follow.

"Dorsch," Kegel said. Dorsch turned to him as Kegel walked over. Kegel moved close to him to speak confidentially. "I spoke to the Führer."

Dorsch was impressed, his eyes widened. "What did he say?"

Kegel swelled for a moment, keeping Dorsch hanging. "He asked me to please be patient. And to please ask you to be patient too. He said, 'Kegel, believe me, I'll be through with my memoirs before you can say Götterdämmerung.'"

Kegel let Dorsch absorb that, then added, "It was touching. There were tears in the Führer's eyes."

Dorsch marveled. Without a word, he turned to head toward Hi, who stood waiting outside of Gebäude Vier.

Kegel turned toward Gebäude Ein, then thought of something else. "Dorsch!" he called. Dorsch stopped and turned again.

"At Munitions, pick us up some more marbles."

10

Gebäude Vier

STURMBANNFÜHRER FRANKEL was doing paperwork as Dorsch brought Hi into the Weinberg. It was the first time Hi had been in Gebäude Vier, and he was intent to note every detail. He could have attended a couple of Kegel's grisly water shows there, but, when told the nature of them, Hi had passed up the chance. He had a good excuse to stay away from some unlucky guy's "dip in the pool": too much work to do in Gebäude Drei on the memoirs.

A meticulous record keeper, Frankel kept a cluttered desk. At the desk behind Frankel's sat Oberschütze Spitz, doing more paperwork still. Near at hand on a table were vials, syringes, and other supplies used in blood work and in dealing with delirium. As Hi, with Dorsch close behind, walked to Frankel's desk with his box of seedlings, he noted the row of barred cells extending into the darkness beyond the desk area's lamplight.

"Schütze Hickenlooper," Frankel greeted him.

"Oberschütze," Hi proudly corrected him.

"Already?"

"Where do you want your Dracaena palm?"

"My what?"

"I'm delivering plants."

Hi was startled to hear a captive wail loudly, deliriously, in one of the far cells in the dark. Spitz promptly got up and took a vial and syringe from the table. Frankel tiredly rose too, picking up his flashlight, as Spitz headed toward the cell while the wailing continued.

"I hate this place," Dorsch said with disgust. "Take Hickenlooper to the Weinkellar next," he told Frankel, who was about to follow Spitz with the light, "then direct him to Munitions."

"Very good, sir."

"I'm going over there now to pick up some—munitions." Hi wondered what for. Frankel was already on his way to help Spitz deal with the delirious captive.

"I *hate* this place," Dorsch said as he left.

Hi found himself alone at the desks, and quickly made the most of it. Setting his seedlings on Frankel's desk, Hi grabbed a syringe and a vial from the table, slipping them into a pocket. Seeing two empty vials in Spitz's wastebasket, Hi retrieved them and pocketed them too.

He glanced around and saw nothing else that was useful. He then began walking curiously, sadly along the cell block, the noise continuing toward the far end. Through the bars he could dimly make out a fitfully sleeping Amazonas Indian, a hapless *caboclo* with a vacant stare, and... Hi couldn't believe his straining eyes. On his bunk in the darkness lay an acquaintance and rival, John Crowley, weak and bearded, head raised with effort, staring back at him.

"Crowley," Hi whispered.

"Hickenlooper." Crowley's eyes gleamed with hope, but then Crowley suddenly looked anxious, he wanted something understood. "We beat you to it," he said. "We found this place first."

"Hang on, pal," Hi said encouragingly. "I'm going to have all of you out of here in about ninety days. Can you make it?"

Crowley's head fell back onto the bunk. "I'll be a ninety-day wonder if I do."

"You can make it. See ya later."

The wailing had stopped, and Frankel and his aide returned. After placing one of the seedlings on the supply table, Frankel escorted Hi into the Weinkellar.

Müller was capping the second of two bottles of blood at a receiving counter, where pipes through the wall brought in extracted blood from the Weinberg.

"Obersturmbannführer," Frankel said, as Müller took the bottles from the counter, "our Yankee friend has a plant for you."

"A plant?" Müller asked with disinterest, glancing at Hi's seedlings, as Frankel helpfully took one of the bottles.

"The dragon's palm," Hi said brightly, "the house plant of vampires." Müller and Frankel took the bottles to the refrigerator, which Frankel opened. The gasoline generator powering the refrigerator could be heard running by the outside wall. "Where would you like me to put it?" Hi's eyes followed the blood as he spoke.

Müller turned to Hi after the bottles had been put into the refrigerator, Frankel closing it. Müller nodded toward a counter by the fridge. "There, I suppose."

Hi took his box to the counter. "You're really going to love your Dracaena," he said, taking a seedling from the box. "When it's bigger you'll see. It's a beautiful palm." Hi sat it proudly on the counter.

"I can't wait to see it," Müller said dryly.

Müller gazed at the seedling as the Sturmbannführer escorted Hi out. He stepped to the counter for a close, careful look. Müller was suspicious by nature. And he suspected something here.

If he only knew what to suspect.

11

Der Rottenführer

HI HAD BEEN IN GEBÄUDE DREI almost nightly, on his editing chores, and had noticed the door to Munitions. It was not far down the corridor from Hi's workplace—a large storage room where Hitler's memoirs were kept, stacked on shelves and a work table. Next door to this room was the Neuanfang maintenance department, under the Hauptsturmführer's supervision. There Schützes worked nightly at carpentry and whatever else was necessary to keep the place up. Kegel's quarters, for example, often needed new panels, though no one seemed to know why. Dorsch himself would come in and get them. The hammering and other noise in maintenance would have bothered Hi next door if he were actually working, but he only glanced through Hitler's work to kill time. No real work was needed, since Hitler had but three months left if things went as planned. And Hi wanted to protect himself mentally. Hitler's memoirs were a mesmerizingly mindrotting read. For several seconds one night, after reading ten pages, Hi couldn't figure out where he was.

Needing no directions from Frankel, Hi headed for Munitions with his box of seedlings. On the way he dropped off a plant at maintenance. The plaque on the Munitions door read MUNITION UND ALLE TAKTISCHE AUFRÜSTUNG (Munitions and All Tactical Armament) or MATA ("kill" in Portuguese and Spanish). Hi knocked on the door and entered.

Hi found Munitions to be a large room with a surprising array of small weaponry and equipment, from hand grenades to bazookas, from boots to frogman outfits, piled on tables and shelves in no discernible overall order. Some order apparently existed, though, as the SS officer present, with a clipboard in hand, was busy doing inventory.

As Hi walked toward the officer, he noted one item that he needed and was definitely going to steal when he could. As for the young officer, Hi had not met him before, and Hi could tell before he got to him that the meeting would be an unpleasant experience.

The officer was a Rottenführer (corporal), about six feet tall and wiry, with a face that, though pale, would be handsome were it capable of smiling or expressing any degree of kind thought. He looked frowningly at the box of seedlings as Hi walked up to him.

"What is this?" the Nazi wanted to know.

"I'm delivering plants."

"Get them out of here." The Rottenführer went back to his clipboard.

"The Führer," Hi said, "wants these plants all around." The Rottenführer threw down the clipboard. "Shall I tell him you—"

"I *said* give them here." The Nazi tried to take the box from Hi's hands.

"You can only have one plant," Hi said, refusing to let go of the box.

"I want the whole box." The Rottenführer pulled on it.

"You can't have it," Hi said, pulling back.

"Give it here." There was a tug-of-war for the box.

"I'm in charge of these plants."

"Give me this box."

"No. You can't—"

The Rottenführer suddenly stopped pulling, but didn't let go. He was looking Hi hard in the eye. "What is your rank?"

So, Hi thought, the guy's pulling rank on me. Hi let go of the box. "Oberschütze," he said. The Rottenführer almost smiled as he held the prize in his hands.

"I'll have to report this," Hi said. "What is *your* rank?"

So, the Nazi thought, he's going to play dirty pool. He handed the box back to Hi. "Rottenführer," he said grudgingly.

"*Rotten*führer?" Hi said. "Talk about qualified." Hi took a seedling from the box and held it out to him. "Here's your plant."

The Rottenführer snatched it out of Hi's hand. He set it, just carefully enough not to break the pot, on the nearest table, and then picked up his clipboard. Turning his back on Hi, he resumed his work.

As Hi turned to leave, the Rottenführer, eyes on his clipboard, said, "I won't forget this, Oberschütze."

Hi, walking toward the door, passed the item he wanted to steal—a gas mask—and stole it, slipping it into his box, without breaking stride. "You just keep track of this inventory," Hi shot back over his shoulder, "and everything'll be all right."

12

Operation Newfangled

EDGAR HICKENLOOPER COULDN'T BELIEVE what he was hearing. He had no reason to doubt the word of Diego Vara, who sat there calmly before him in the den of Edgar's Florida mansion. And the last cryptic message from Hi, a month earlier, had prepared the food magnate for something extraordinary—Hi, said the telegram, was embarking on a secret four-month expedition that would be explained later, that could not be allowed to fail, and that Edgar must materially support. Yet Diego's story was all but beyond credulity. Edgar was almost hyperventilating as he paced.

"My son Hiram a vampire? But he's never been in trouble before. Now he's running around with Hitler?"

"All according to plan," Diego quietly reiterated. "If it works, Mr. Hickenlooper, your son will be the greatest unsung hero of the twentieth century, if not of all time."

"I just wanted him to find some damn city." Edgar tried to calm down. "What do you need from me?"

"Garlic powder." Edgar gaped at Diego. Was this a practical joke after all? "Garlic flowers are a vampire repellent. Enough powder will confuse, temporarily incapacitate—we hope."

Edgar sighed. "My son a vampire." Then, remembering something, he looked urgently at Diego. "This vampire cure—you say there's a cure?"

"Yes. We think so." Diego chuckled.
"Why are you laughing?"
"Wait till you hear what it is."

Edgar delivered the goods. One month after his talk with Diego, a DC6 cargo plane, full of nothing but stacked boxes of Hickenlooper Foods garlic powder, landed on the airstrip at Canutama, Brazil. McKay himself watched the DC6 land, as did a shirtless, muscular IQ contract pilot who was holding a paintbrush. The pilot was painting insignia on the nose of a crop duster, one of three that were parked by the jungle strip. One duster already sported a feisty little fire-breathing dragon on its nose, with the caption DUSTY DRAGON. On the nose of the second duster the pilot was presently painting a caricature of himself, grinning and bent over, his bared butt blowing out garlic powder. The caption would be EAT MY DUST.

Operation Newfangled—as Hi, Diego, and McKay had named what McKay called "our plan" on that last planning night in Manaus—called for the three crop dusters to deliver the "dust" over Hitler's lair at sunrise on the one hundred and twentieth day. McKay, Diego, and a team of war-hardened commandos would then hit the compound.

But the hope was that, by the time Hi got through at Neuanfang on the one hundred and nineteenth night, the garlic powder and commandos would not even be needed.

Part Three
Dragon's Blood

1

First Blood

ON THE ONE HUNDRED and nineteenth day of Operation Newfangled, Hi arose from his coffin. It was almost mid-morning. He had tried to sleep for a couple of hours, since a hard night's day lay ahead of him.

On the table, what had once been a Dracaena palm seedling was a full-grown plant. And if Doctor Po had been right, it would have a stemful of dragon's blood. So it was time to rehearse what Hi had to do that day at various points on the compound: extract the lethal nectar. He had to hope he would have enough of it, and that meant tapping every plant that he could. Assuming, of course, that there was something to extract. Hi was confident that there would be. He had raised perfect-looking plants. But he knew Murphy's Law—if something can go wrong, it will—and he expected to encounter it, perhaps more than once, before sunrise tomorrow.

Hi took his syringe and a vial from the loose lining of his coffin where he had hidden them, and set them on the table. He rubbed his hands together, then rubbed them on his black shirt, as he nervously regarded the plant. It was make-or-break time. Picking up the syringe, he carefully stuck its needle into the stem of the plant. He then pulled slowly on the plunger to extract what was there. This was not a dry run, of course, because every drop counted. And it worked. The barrel of the syringe nearly half-filled with the Dracaena palm's bright red secretion.

"I could kiss you, Po," Hi said.

He transferred the liquid into the vial. The vial was still more than half empty. Taking two more vials from the coffin, he put the vials in his pockets. Slightly loosening his tucked-in shirt, he hid the syringe inside of it. He adjusted the vials to make the bulges as unnoticeable as possible in his SS breeches. Then Hi turned toward the door, steeled himself, and walked quietly out of Gebäude Zwei.

He headed first for the Weinberg. In his four months at Neuanfang, Hi had become a familiar sight, going about to check on his plants as they steadily grew, and to work (supposedly) on the memoirs stored in Gebäude Drei. So Hi moved freely on the compound in the performance of his duties. But moving about in the day could easily draw attention, whatever the purpose. It was like prowling at night in the land of the living. And though Hi didn't know it, on this crucial occasion he drew the attention of Müller, who was sitting up late, clad only in his underwear, reading a book entitled *Health Care in Your Amazon Home*, at the window of his Gebäude Ein quarters.

Müller wondered why Hi, at this time of day, was going into Gebäude Vier.

Müller got up to dress and find out.

2

Caught in the Act

REMER, A YOUNG BLONDE OBERSCHÜTZE, was sitting back, eyes closed, half-dozing, his feet propped on the aide's desk, when Hi walked into the Weinberg. The dark cell block was silent except for one person moaning. As Hi moved quietly toward the Dracaena palm sitting gloriously on the table near the desk, he hoped the Oberschütze's nodding would turn to sound sleep. But it didn't. Seeing Hi, Remer quickly took his feet off the desk and sat up.

"Relax, pal," Hi said as he stepped to the table. "I couldn't sleep, so I thought I'd check on the plants."

Remer relaxed again, returning his feet to the desk top and locking his hands behind his head. Hi's back was to Remer, who couldn't see Hi slip the syringe out of the front of his shirt.

"I tried not to disturb you," Hi said. "How long have they had you on the graveyard shift?"

"Too long." Hi stuck the syringe needle into the plant stem. Remer, trying to stay awake, was not even looking toward Hi. "It is hard to imagine, your being unable to sleep."

Hi began extracting the dragon's blood with the plunger. "Well, I haven't been a vampire for long," Hi said. "I'm still learning all the ins and outs. It's hard to get used to the hours."

"You're telling me?"

Hi slipped the roughly half-filled syringe back into his shirt. Turning from the table, he saw Remer had his eyes closed. "I'm going to check the palm next door, okay?" Remer nodded without opening his eyes.

As Hi walked through the shadows to the Weinkellar door, he looked toward Crowley's cell to his right. Hi couldn't tell in the dark if Crowley was still there.

Entering the Weinkellar, Hi closed the door behind him. He stepped over to the open door of the small office and looked inside. Müller wasn't there. Hi then hurried to the fridge. He opened it and saw three full bottles of blood. Closing it, Hi turned quickly to the Dracaena palm on the counter. Once he had its extract he could go ahead and put all that he had so far into the three bottles of blood, which he was confident were for consumption that evening. Even if Hi couldn't get back to put in some more extract before the midnight meal, what he had would be better than nothing. Taking the syringe from his shirt, Hi first began emptying its contents into a vial.

Meanwhile Müller walked into the Weinberg. He found Oberschütze Remer sound asleep. Müller would deal with him later. For the moment the Obersturmbannführer looked toward the Weinkellar.

Hi was in the act of extracting dragon's blood from the palm when the door opened and Müller walked in. Hearing him enter, Hi yanked the syringe from the plant and hid it behind his back as he turned. But trying to hide the instrument was futile, for Müller had glimpsed it.

Müller swaggered over to Hi, who smiled, the syringe still behind his back. Hi wondered what to do as Müller, hands clasped behind his back, cockily stood there and rocked on his heels, waiting for an explanation. Hi's first impulse was to stick Müller between the eyes and pump in the juice. But that, too, would have been hard to explain.

"Tell me, Herr Hickenlooper," Müller said, "what is it about your plants?"

"What is it?" repeated Hi, as if the question were dumb, though he still didn't know how to answer. He knew he'd have to start with the truth. Still smiling, he took the syringe from behind his back. "The extract," he said. "Looks like you've caught me red-handed."

Müller, lips pursed, looked at the syringe in Hi's hand, then waited for Hi's further explanation.

"But I'll make a deal with you," Hi told him in a confidential tone. Gesturing with the syringe, he said, "Wanna try some?"

Hi saw the expression change in Müller's eyes. He could see that Müller was catching on. That is, Müller *thought* he was catching on.

"How about tonight?" Hi asked encouragingly. "You know the best time? Just before dinner. It takes a few hours to hit you."

Müller looked tempted. But still suspicious.

"What's it called?" Müller asked.

"Uh—Dracaena palm extract. DPE. That's—'dope' in English." Hi chuckled at the ad-libbed acronym. Müller looked at him curiously. "Don't worry," Hi assured him. "Non-addictive."

Müller considered, his eyes shifting back and forth between the syringe in Hi's hand and Hi's eyes.

"Pretty good stuff, eh?" asked Müller.

"'Pretty good'?" Hi almost laughed. "It'll blow the top of your head off."

3

Sex, Dope, and Slang

AFTER MAKING A DEAL with Müller, Hi proceeded to Gebäude Drei. Though Müller's meddling had prevented Hi from spiking the blood in the Weinkellar fridge, Müller was unwittingly giving him a second chance at it. For Hi had an invitation to return to the Weinkellar at eleven that evening—an hour before mealtime—so that Müller might partake of Hi's extract. If it proved to be as mindblowing as Hi claimed, Müller agreed that the nectar would be kept secret for his and Hi's exclusive enjoyment. If the secret of the extract got out, Müller said, the Schützes would keep the Dracaenas sucked dry.

In Gebäude Drei, Hi extracted more liquid ammo from the palm in the maintenance department, where no one was around, and then from the one next door in his workplace. He found the Munitions door locked, and though Hi knocked, he was sure the Rottenführer was asleep in Gebäude Zwei. Hi would have to do without the Rottenführer's Dracaena. He doubted he could have extracted anything anyway had the officer been there. Though making a Müller-type deal with him might be easy, the Rottenführer, being the bootlicker he was, more likely would go straight to the Führer.

Hi was also concerned, as he left Gebäude Drei, about still having no gas masks for Eva and the Countess. Before the next sunrise they would both have to be off of the compound. There was no telling what the garlic powder—which Hi prayed was loaded and ready for takeoff at Canutama—would do to an unprotected vampire.

Hi headed for the Countess's next, via the Gebäude Ein rear door. If seen in Gebäude Ein by SS, Hi could only say he was tending the plants. As Hi explained to her the effect of Dracaena palm extract—DPE or "dope," he now called it—the Countess watched him tap the dragon's blood from her Dracaena. "And to think," she said, "I kept one for years in my castle."

After telling the Countess to be sure she didn't touch any blood that night, and to get off of the compound before sunrise, Hi gave her a kiss on the cheek, and proceeded to Eva's quarters.

Hi and Eva embraced and kissed passionately. They had waited for this time alone for four months. Hi needed to tap that Dracaena, but Eva, pulling him toward her rosewood coffin, begged him to tap her first. Hi could never say no to her. They made love in the coffin, its gold handles rattling. If seen by SS, Hi could only say it was worth it. When they finished, Eva smoked a cigarette while Hi poked the plant with his instrument.

"Remember," Hi said, extracting, "no blood tonight."

"No blood," she said languidly.

"Be ready to get going, you and the Countess, about an hour before dawn."

Crushing out her cigarette in the Dracaena palm pot, Eva put her arms around Hi as he emptied the syringe into a vial. "Hi, please be careful tonight."

Hi was concerned. "I could use some more, Eva."

"You've got it. Let's get back in the coffin."

"No, I mean some more dragon's blood. What if I don't have enough? What if they just puke or get diarrhea?"

"We can't think about that. Let's get back in the coffin."

No, Hi was going to tap one more plant. And it wasn't just because he worried about having enough—though that justified taking the risk. If the dragon's blood worked, Hi wanted the irony and satisfaction of having at least one drop from Hitler's own plant, Neuanfang's prize palm.

"Let's hope the Führer's a sound sleeper," Hi said, putting the syringe back into his shirt.

"You're going to tap his?" Eva fearfully held onto him. "Hi, no! A Schütze is guarding his quarters."

"I'll have to get around him."

"What if he wakes up and catches you?"

"The Schütze?"

"Hitler, you galoot." She had picked up that slang word from a Randolph Scott western.

"If he wakes up, I guess we're kaput. Don't worry, I'll be on my toes. I'll think of something to say. Like what, I don't know."

They looked into each other's eyes. Hi loved her so much he could be tempted just to fly away with her now, if she tried to persuade him. But Hi had a job to do. And he didn't even know yet how to turn himself into a bat. He had been meaning to ask.

"Quick. How do I turn myself into a bat?"

She was unprepared for the question. "It's not easy to explain. It's like learning to ride a bicycle. You, uh—"

"Forget it, show me later." Hi took her in his arms. "Besides, if Hitler wakes up, could I fly off and leave you?"

"No, you couldn't," she informed him. "Vampires can't fly in the day."

"That's right, I forgot. Well, I wouldn't if I could."

They shared a long, gentle kiss. "No matter what happens," he said softly, "remember this..." He tried to think of something less trite than "I love you," but he couldn't spend much time on it. "I really dig you, Eva."

She knew that English slang too. They kissed again, as if for the last time.

"Oh Hi," she said, before letting him go. "You're the most."

4

"Don't Lick It"

OBERGRUPPENFÜHRER KEGEL couldn't sleep. He decided to make a round of the compound. If he couldn't sleep, no one on duty was going to sleep either. Kegel stepped out of his quarters not more than five seconds after Hi had eased past. Hi, not hearing Kegel come out, was then going up the stairway, unheard by Kegel, to head for Hitler's quarters.

Kegel thought for a moment. He should start by going upstairs to check on Schütze Bingle, who was guarding Hitler's quarters. But first Kegel wanted to aggravate the Countess, if she happened to be awake. If she was asleep, he could contemplate her nice face and at least imagine the rest of her.

The Countess, in white nightgown, wasn't sleepy. As Kegel walked in without knocking, he found her lying propped on an elbow in her coffin reading a dog-eared paperback called *Hemophilia*.

"Still here, I see," Kegel smiled.

"I'm escaping tomorrow." She boredly turned a page and kept reading.

Kegel chuckled. "Over my undead body," he said, as he strolled over to her Dracaena. She watched him from the corner of her eye.

Something on the plant's stem grabbed Kegel's attention. He looked closer. It was a small, drying trickle of red liquid, from what appeared to be, as he looked even closer, a very small hole in the stem.

"This plant is bleeding!"

"Call the doctor," she said dryly, pretending to read. She hadn't noticed any residue, and was trying to think what to say.

With a rub Kegel smeared some of the liquid onto his finger and looked at it. Then he looked at the Countess. Call the doctor my ass, Kegel thought. Müller was the closest thing at Neuanfang to a doctor. Vampires, they had found, have few ailments, none terminal. And this plant called for no doctor. It called for an explanation, and Kegel waited for the Countess to supply it.

She looked over at him, staring at her as he held the finger with the smear near his face.

"I confess," she said, tossing aside her book. "I've been doing DPE."

"Doing what?" He watched her climb out of the coffin.

"Dracaena palm extract. Why do you think I kept a Dracaena all those years in my castle?" She walked casually over to Kegel. "There's nothing like 'dope,' Obergruppenführer."

He looked at the red smear on his finger. She was afraid he was going to lick it. If Kegel died before all the others, it could ruin the timing of Hi's operation, if not give it away completely.

Kegel looked at her and smiled. He opened his mouth, put out his tongue, and raised his finger toward it.

"Don't lick it," she said. Kegel looked at her quizzically, the finger an inch from his mouth. "Some vampires," she said nervously, "have an allergic reaction."

"What happens?"

"They . . . explode."

Kegel looked at her, not knowing whether to believe

her or not. "You're full of it."

"I see you've been talking to Dorsch."

Kegel looked again at the plant. "What do you get it out with? A syringe?"

"Yes." She began looking at Kegel seductively. "Don't tell anyone. It'll be our secret—our DPE..."

Kegel liked how she said it. "Hickenlooper doesn't know?" he asked.

"That idiot? He thinks they're just pretty plants." She playfully ran a finger around on the Nazi's chest. "If just you and I share, you can... come and see me whenever you want it."

"The DPE?"

She smiled coyly. "That too."

Kegel was already getting a hard-on. He knew she hated him, he knew she was playing up to him only to protect herself and her dope. But that was good enough for Kegel. He tried to embrace her, but she gently resisted. "What's your blood type?" she asked.

"My blood type? I don't know. What—"

"Type O's have allergic reaction," she explained. "Otherwise you're okay. Have Müller get your blood type. But don't tell him why." She smiled again, sweetly. "Then come back and see me tomorrow. And we'll do it."

"You mean—"

"That too." She stepped close to him, put her hand on the bulge in his breeches, and gently squeezed. "Bring this bugger back with you."

5

Bingle the Dingle

SCHÜTZE BINGLE, with a Mauser strapped to his shoulder, was pacing quietly that morning in front of the closed door to Hitler's quarters. Thirty-seven years old, Bingle was short and solidly built, with black hair, slightly crossed eyes, and a gap between his two front teeth. He almost enjoyed daytime sentry duty, especially when it meant guarding the Führer. The day shift gave Bingle time to think, and it beat flying around on bat patrol in the evening. Right now Bingle was thinking about last Saturday night at the Gebäude Vier conversion pool. All that billowing blood and teeth clattering. He sure hoped there would be another show soon.

At about the same moment that Kegel was entering the Countess's quarters downstairs, Hi, having ascended to the second floor, peeked down the corridor from the corner of the stairway landing. He saw that the sentry guarding Hitler's suite was the Schütze named Bingle with the dental hollow. Hi called him Bingle the Dingle. Hi stayed hidden for a few moments, thinking how best to handle him. Hi figured it wouldn't be hard. Surely Bingle would take a good bribe, and Hi had a doozy to offer.

Bingle was facing in the other direction as Hi emerged from the stairway. Turning, the Schütze suddenly became alert, questioningly watching as Hi, with that little spring in his gait, came walking toward him.

Hi stepped up to Bingle and smiled. "I guess the Führer's asleep," Hi whispered. The Nazi just stared without answering. Hi wondered at that moment if he was making a mistake, taking too big a chance to try to tap Hitler's plant. But he forged ahead. "How long have you been in this place?" Hi whispered amiably.

Bingle looked at his watch. "About four hours," he whispered.

"No. I mean how long in the jungle."

"I date back to day one of the first Neuanfang. Seven years."

"Seven years and still a Schütze?"

Bingle shrugged. "They say they need me where I am. What the hell, I've got centuries. That's why I signed up. I feel okay about it."

"Well, I'll tell you what," Hi said with a mischievous smile. "I can make you feel a lot better."

Bingle reared back from him slightly.

"No, you don't understand," Hi said. He proceeded to offer Bingle a regular supply of DPE, even telling him that Müller was in on the deal. The three of them would share the secret of the dragon's palm, enjoy its euphoriant nectar, non-addictive, as long as the plants would produce. Müller would get his that evening, Hi explained, but Hi would take care of Bingle soon after. All Bingle had to do was let Hi slip in while Hitler slept and get some of the dope. Hitler had the best plant, its DPE would be out of this world. Bingle frowned, thoughtfully pressing his tongue against the gap in his teeth. He could sure use some of that DPE stuff. A continuous supply? Almost too good to be true. "What if the Führer wakes up," he asked, "while you're in there?"

Hi shrugged. "I'll tell him I couldn't sleep and was checking on the plants."

"And I let you in?"

"I pulled rank on you. I'll tell him that I told you the damn plant would die if I didn't see it today. Were you going to let the Führer's plant die?"

"No, I couldn't do that," Bingle said, still frowning.

"You see? There's no problem." Hi held up two crossed fingers in Bingle's face. "The Führer and I are like *that*." Smiling at Bingle, Hi eased open Hitler's door and went in, quietly closing it behind him.

Hitler was sleeping in his white pajamas in the open coffin. It was across the room from his desk. On the table near the center of the room was the magnificent red-flowered palm.

Hi regarded Hitler for a moment, with loathing. He thought about how nice, how easy it would be, if he had a hammer and stake, to go over and dispatch the bastard right then. But Hi was not on a suicide mission. His task was clearcut: eradicate these vermin, but get Eva, the Countess, the captives, and himself safely out. That meant patience for a little while longer. And not being discovered. Contrary to the spiel he gave Bingle, Hi still didn't know, as he stealthily proceeded to the table, what he'd say—as if anything could save him—should Hitler wake up. Hitler was no Bingle the Dingle, and Hi didn't even want to think about getting caught by the Führer.

The extraction went fine. Hitler slept, and the dragon's blood from the plant filled half the syringe. As Hi put the syringe back into his shirt, he felt confident that he had enough juice. For good measure he planned to tap, if he could, the Dracaena in the main hall, on his way out of Gebäude Ein. For extra good measure, he would hit the one in the Gebäude Zwei drink hall, just before getting back to his room. In his room he would wait for his return that night, with vials full of DPE, to Müller's Weinkellar.

Müller was the one obstacle left.

Or so Hi thought.

As he started to turn from Hitler's Dracaena, Hi noticed that some extract residue had oozed from the hole left by the needle, and was trickling down the plant stem. Concerned, he wondered if other plants he had tapped did the same. If they did, he hoped no one had noticed. No one would know the red secretion's significance—but that was the trouble: some curious Nazi could ingest it prematurely and die, leaving Hi with some explaining to do about this previously unmentioned secretion.

Intending to find something to wipe off the stem with, Hi turned to look around—and was startled to see Kegel standing in the doorway, staring at him. Looking over Kegel's shoulder was hapless Bingle the Dingle, with terror in his slightly crossed eyes.

6

Bad Dreams

KEGEL, KEEPING HIS EYES ON HI, gloated as he strode over to Hitler's coffin. Bending over his sleeping leader, Kegel gently squeezed his arm and said quietly, "Mein Führer." Hitler's eyes opened, and looked up blankly at Kegel. "I am sorry to disturb you, but it seems our intruder," Kegel said, gesturing toward Hi, "has once again intruded."

Raising his head, Hitler glowered at Hi, who still stood, at a loss, by the table. "I just caught him," Kegel told the Führer with great satisfaction, "here in your quarters."

The frowning Führer began getting out of the coffin. Hi frantically searched his mind as he waited to be grilled. He wished he was dreaming all this. Then the wish gave Hi an idea.

"My robe," Hitler said hoarsely. Kegel fetched it from a peg and helped Hitler into it. Tying the belt, Hitler walked over to Hi, standing contritely by the table, and crossed his arms on his chest. Hitler cocked back his head and stared down his nose at Hi. "First," said the Führer, "how did you get past Schütze Bingle?"

Hi glanced at Bingle, who was looking on terrified from the doorway. Kegel, stepping to Hitler's side, looked smugly at Hi and leaned forward, as if eager to hear Hi's explanation.

Hi hesitated, as if about to confess some horrible misdeed. "I explained to him that you were in danger," Hi finally told Hitler. "He had to let me in to confirm it."

"That's right, mein Führer!" scared Bingle exclaimed from the doorway. "I had to know if you were in danger!"

Hitler closed his eyes in forbearance, fists clenched under his folded arms, lips pressed tightly shut under his Charlie Chaplin moustache. After a moment he opened his eyes again and looked at Hi. "In danger from what?" he asked in a quiet, controlled tone.

Hi sighed remorsefully, seeming almost near tears. "Mein Führer, I've made a terrible mistake." Hi gestured toward the Dracaena palm. "I should *never* have brought these plants here. Can you ever forgive me?"

Hitler frowned with concern and impatience. "What are you talking about, Oberschütze?"

"I had a dream, mein Führer, a nightmare," Hi said with anguish, putting both hands to his head as he began pacing about. "I dreamt that the dragon's palm produces a secretion—called, in this nightmare, dragon's blood—that is lethal, even to vampires. I dreamt that Herr Kegel stood here and, in honor of you, held a cup to this, your own dragon's palm, as it poured dragon's blood from its stem. The Obergruppenführer drank it, and—and *exploded*, filling your quarters, mein Führer, with a thousand bloody pieces of himself." Hi seemed choked with emotion.

"Get to the point," Hitler growled. Kegel was listening to Hi with amazement. Here again was talk of vampires exploding.

"I woke up, in a cold sweat," Hi said, almost gasping for breath, "and I saw it, on the plant in my room. I saw dragon's blood oozing out of the stem"—Hi put a hand to his throat as if he would strangle—"as if it was ready to spew out and attack me, seeping into my pores, and—"

"Nonsense!" Hitler said, stepping closer to Hi. "Pull yourself together, Oberschütze. It was a dream, it—"

"No, mein Führer," Hi said half-hysterically, "the dream was an omen. Look!" Hi pointed at the stem of Hitler's Dracaena. "It is real, mein Führer. I ran here to see—to see if dragon's blood was coming out of your plant, endangering you. And look! there it is!"

Hitler looked. Sure enough, there was bloodlike red liquid on the Dracaena palm's stem.

"We've got to destroy them, mein Führer," Hi said urgently, "we've got to destroy all of these plants! They're endangering everyone on the compound!"

"Nonsense!" Kegel said. "You heard the Führer. It was only a dream."

"But see here, Kegel," the confused Führer said, pointing at the plant stem. "There *is*, uh—dragon's blood or whatever, on this plant."

"Mein Führer," Kegel said quietly, "may I have a word with you?"

Hitler followed Kegel over toward the coffin, away from Hi, who continued acting distraught. Kegel was not about to let his and the Countess's DPE supply be destroyed. "There is nothing wrong with the plants," Kegel whispered to Hitler. "This imbecile has it all wrong."

Hitler looked quizzically at Kegel. "How can you be sure? There *are* such things as omens. If he dreamed—"

"He *thought* he was dreaming," Kegel said, no longer whispering. "He woke up from a dream, and, half-asleep, saw his damn plant was bleeding, and thought he had dreamed it. He had actually dreamed something else."

"But the plant *was* bleeding—that's the point," Hitler said in full voice. "Who cares what he dreamed? To be on the safe side, we destroy the plants, and—"

"Mein Führer," Kegel politely interrupted, "may I have another word with you?" Kegel and Hitler moved still further away from Hi. Kegel knew why the plant was bleeding: obviously the Countess had tapped Hitler's plant. Kegel wouldn't presume to ask Hitler what the Countess had been doing in his quarters. Kegel was perfectly willing to share her.

"I've been meaning to tell you," Kegel whispered. "I only recently found out myself." Noting Bingle still in the doorway, Kegel ordered him out with a nod of the head. Kegel then glanced back at Hi—who was wondering what Kegel was up to—to be sure Hi couldn't hear.

"What he calls dragon's blood," Kegel whispered to Hitler, "this Dracaena palm extract, is a drug. A non-addictive narcotic." Hitler looked at Kegel with amazement. Kegel whispered more quietly still, "I need not tell you, mein Führer, the potential—"

"Could you speak a little louder?" Hitler whispered. Hi wondered what the hell they were saying.

"Of course." Kegel put his arm around Hitler's shoulders, and whispered right in his ear. "You can see the potential such a substance has, if produced in sufficient quantity, both for large revenues and for—bribery enhancement." Hitler liked what he was hearing. "A fringe benefit to offer all deserving allies or minions."

"Yes," Hitler said, intrigued. "For their eternal enjoyment." Then he looked curiously at Kegel. "How do you know this?"

"Know what?"

"Remove your arm, please."

Kegel took his arm from Hitler's shoulders. "Forgive me, mein Führer." Kegel was trying to think of an answer to Hitler's question.

"How do you know this secret of the dragon's blood? That it is a non-addictive narcotic."

Kegel couldn't tell him the truth. If Kegel implicated

the Countess, he would lose her promised affections. Kegel needed to implicate someone he would like to lose altogether. "Dorsch told me," he said.

"Dorsch? How did *he* know?"

"I should have asked. I'll ask him as soon as I see him. In fact, I'll go wake him up now."

Kegel left in a hurry, to talk to Dorsch before Hitler had a chance to.

Hitler mused for a moment. If Dorsch knew, what difference did the *how* make? The Führer felt good as he walked over to Hi. He was appreciative of Hi's great concern, however misguided, and of the unforeseen benefit Hi's plants had brought for the future.

"You've done it again, Oberschütze," Hitler said cheerily.

"I have?" Hi wondered what in the world Kegel had told him.

"You think this blood of the dragon could harm me. But the joke is on you." Hitler chuckled.

Hi smiled nervously. "How is that?"

"You may be told in due course. The important thing now is, you must nurture more plants." Hitler spoke amiably but firmly. "You must fill Gebäude Zwei and Gebäude Drei with them. Do you understand? You must give us that dragon's blood."

"I understand."

"The more you can give us, the better."

"I'll give you as much as I can."

Hitler smiled. "You will dine here this evening, with me and the officers."

Oh great, Hi thought, so I'm going to die after all.

7

Two Bound for Hell

AT ELEVEN O'CLOCK THAT NIGHT, Hi went to the Weinberg. He went armed with three vials full of DPE in his pockets. Upon leaving Hitler's quarters that day, he had tapped the palm in the Gebäude Ein main hall, and then the one in the Gebäude Zwei drink hall, on the way to his room. If that still wasn't enough, so be it. He had given it his best shot. His last remaining task was to get what he had into the Weinkellar blood supply for the compound's midnight meal—then avoid drinking any blood himself as a guest at Hitler's table. That invitation was yet another unforeseen complication. If Hi simply didn't show up for his nightly glass of blood in the Gebäude Zwei drink hall, no one would take much notice. But he would need a damn good excuse to turn down drinking with Hitler.

Hi spent most of the early evening in the Gebäude Drei storage room—ostensibly working on the memoirs—thinking about how not to drink any blood without possibly arousing some suspicion in Hitler and the others. Short of not showing up, he could think of only one thing to do.

But first there was Müller to deal with. When he walked into the Weinberg at eleven, Hi found Oberschütze Spitz working busily at his desk. Hi nodded hello as Spitz glanced up from his paperwork. Gesturing toward the Weinkellar, Spitz said simply, "They are expecting you, Hickenlooper," and continued to work.

Hi looked calm, but inside he felt panic. Who were "they"? Had Müller set him up? Was Kegel in there? What had Hitler and Kegel whispered about? Spitz, wondering why Hi hadn't moved yet, looked up at him.

"Have *they* been here long?" Hi asked casually.

"For most of the evening," Spitz said. He went back to his work.

Hi turned and walked toward the Weinkellar door, which had a wall lamp next to it, the only light in the Weinberg except for the two desk lamps. Hi felt sure he was walking into more Murphy's Law. He glanced toward Crowley's cell, but could make nothing out in the darkness between the light of the lamps.

Walking into the Weinkellar, Hi found Müller sitting at the desk in his cubby-hole office. There with him, in a chair by the desk, was Sturmbannführer Frankel. Hi was relieved to see no one else. But he wondered why Frankel was there. If the Sturmbannführer was just visiting, why did Spitz say *they* were expecting him?

Frankel rose as Hi walked over. "Good evening, Oberschütze." Hi couldn't tell if the smile on Frankel's face was a false one or not.

"Good evening." Hi looked at Müller, but the Obersturmbannführer just sat there, regarding him, with his usual poker face.

"Here to check on your plant?" asked Frankel, still smiling.

"Yes." Hi didn't know what else to say.

Frankel kept smiling for a moment, but then squinted his eyes accusingly. "You are lying, Oberschütze."

Hi looked again at Müller, who still offered no help. Then Frankel laughed, and slapped Hi chummily on the shoulder.

"I have let Herr Frankel in on our little secret," Müller

said finally. Hi felt great relief. "He has been a loyal and conscientious officer. He wrings every drop of blood that he can from those stinking wretches next door."

"Please, Obersturmbannführer," Frankel said with false modesty, "you embarrass me."

"He deserves a little reward," Müller said.

"Sure," Hi smiled. "Why not?" Frankel stood there smiling and waiting. Hi looked at Müller. "Got the glasses?" Müller opened a desk drawer to get them, while Frankel, rubbing his hands together, sat back down. Hi had told Müller that the extract, being acrid by itself, went down best mixed with blood, which masked its unpleasant taste. Hi had no idea, of course, how the stuff really tasted, with blood or without, and did not intend to find out.

As Müller arranged three glasses and a spoon on the table, Hi took a vial of dragon's blood out of his pocket. Frankel's eyes widened at the sight as Hi held it between finger and thumb.

"In the absence of Oberschütze Spitz," Hi said graciously, tantalizing them with the vial, "allow me to serve as your waiter."

Vial still in hand, Hi turned and headed for the refrigerator, cater-cornered from the office. Frankel crossed his legs and cheerfully called after him, "Your secret is safe with me. But whatever you do"—he was almost stuttering in his anticipation—"do not tell Kegel or Dorsch."

"Hah," Hi called back as he opened the fridge. "I wouldn't tell those guys how to fly." Taking out one of the three bottles of blood, he uncapped it as he went back to the office.

"It's best," Hi said, "to pour one glass from each bottle." He poured Müller's glass first. "That way no one will notice there's a little blood missing."

"Good idea," Müller said. Hi liked the irony of the comment, coming from a man who would kill anyone caught stealing blood.

As Müller and Frankel expectantly watched, Hi carefully poured a dose of the dragon's blood from the vial into Müller's glass of blood. "Stir it up," Hi said, "and then down the hatch." He smiled at Frankel. "You're next, Sturmbannführer."

Hi headed back to the fridge. "Like I said," he called to them over his shoulder, "it'll be a few hours before we feel the effect." At the fridge Hi's back was to the office. Through the office doorway the Nazis couldn't see the fridge anyway without leaning over and craning their necks. Müller and Frankel sat relaxed, unsuspecting. as Hi opened the fridge, set the first bottle back in, and, before capping it, emptied the vial of dragon's blood into the bottle.

As Hi took out the second bottle with one hand, with the other he exchanged the empty vial for a full one from his pocket. With the new vial in hand, he uncapped the second bottle on his way back to the office.

"The nice thing about it," Hi said as he poured Frankel's glass from the bottle, "is that you can't get addicted." He poured a dose of DPE from the vial—the two Nazis thought it the same vial as before, Hi's hand obscuring the fact it was full—into Frankel's glass of blood. "You can use this stuff once, and not have to worry about getting any more."

With the bottle and vial in one hand, Hi picked up the third glass with the other. "Let me get mine," he said, turning toward the fridge, "and we'll toast."

"But if it does all that you say," Frankel said, eagerly stirring his drink with the spoon as Hi went to the fridge, "how can we not help but worry? There is nothing worse than wanting something that you can't have more of."

On his way to the fridge, Hi emptied the second vial into the second bottle in his hand.

"Don't worry," Müller said. "Herr Hickenlooper will see that we get it."

As Hi returned the second bottle to the fridge, he simultaneously exchanged vials once again. He uncapped the third bottle, poured his glass of blood, and set the glass on the counter. He emptied the vial into the bottle as he set it back in the fridge.

Capping the bottle and closing the fridge, Hi picked up his glass of blood and headed back to the office. As he rejoined Müller and Frankel, he showed off the empty vial. "Well, that's it," Hi said, putting the vial into his pocket. Frankel offered Hi the spoon, but Hi was already stirring his blood with a finger. "Oh, I'm sorry," Hi said, acting embarrassed by his crude faux pas. "I'm used to not having a spoon."

"That's all right," Müller said. "From now on you will have one." He raised his glass in a toast. "Heil Hitler."

"Heil Hitler," Hi said.

"Sieg heil," Frankel said, and eagerly began downing his blood. Hi, as he began drinking his own, watched Frankel and thought, So long, sucker. He watched Müller drinking his too. Have fun in hell, Hi thought.

Hi was relieved that neither Nazi detected any bad taste in his blood, since he had already told them they wouldn't. That meant hopefully no one at the midnight meal would taste something strange and suspect tainted blood. And Hi was exhilarated that the tainting had gone so smoothly. Though it remained to be seen how much help he might need, Hi hoped things were going as well for the operation on the outside of Neuanfang as they were—at least for the moment—on the inside.

8

The Eve of Saint George

EVEN AS HI was spiking the blood in the Weinkellar, some two hundred yards away McKay, Diego, and a crack team of commandos, thirty in all, had taken position in the jungle darkness, to await the dawn of the one hundred and twentieth day. They had crept in on foot from Nova Dolencia, arriving soon after sundown, and now waited, tired but eager, in camouflage suits, with gas masks, hammers and stakes, as well as conventional firearms, as a bright moon peaked through the black jungle canopy. With blackened faces and hands, they kept low in the thick undergrowth, moving about as little as possible, and staying a good distance from the edge of the clearing. They had correctly assumed there would be bats—not the natural-born variety—keeping eyes out overhead on the compound's perimeter.

Come morning, with the crop dusters hitting the compound with garlic, McKay's team would descend on Neuanfang for the kill—assuming that Hi with the dragon's blood had not already done the job. The ground assault would coincide with the second of three scheduled passes by the planes. The first garlic bombardment, catching the vampires by surprise, would virtually immobilize them, or spread such havoc that they could easily be done in by the commandos, striking under cover of the second bombardment and reinforced by the third. That, at least, was the plan.

Heading the commandos was a six-foot-four American hulk named Johnny Ringawa. Handpicked by McKay, Ringawa was a World War II legend. He had been the only marine in the Pacific to take a Japanese island all by himself. Or so the headlines had read. Intrepid though he was, he was actually AWOL at the time, on a drunken binge, the Japanese having already left the island. But Ringawa had already proved himself as a leader in combat, and, with the help of the glorifying media, became for a time a Marine Corps poster boy. McKay, upon learning that Ringawa was living and working in Brazil as a B-movie actor (he was sort of Brazil's Audie Murphy), looked him up, and chose him for Operation Newfangled. Ringawa was still in great physical shape, complaining only of a slight trick knee, which he blamed on the bossa nova. McKay knew that the man had his quirks. Ringawa ate only veggies, and as the team sat waiting in the jungle that night, he wore a pink sweatband around his curly blonde locks, and was sporting vilca-wood earrings. "In intelligence work," McKay remarked to Diego, "we have to deal with all kinds."

Lying on his muscular back, Ringawa gazed up at a patch of moon through the canopy. "We found them suckers," he said. "I can't wait till tomorrow." He spoke with a strong Deep South accent, which was odd, since he came from the Bronx.

"Let's hope things go well tonight," Diego said, glancing off in the direction of Neuanfang. "This is it. The night of the dragon's blood."

"You know what I call it?" said Ringawa. "The Eve of Saint George. Hitler's the dragon and us guys and Hick are Saint George."

McKay had found Ringawa increasingly irritating. He was beginning to regret his selection. "Saint George's

Day," McKay informed him, "is April twenty-third."

Ringawa sat up to give the Britisher a look. The rough-hewn yet prim ex-marine had found McKay increasingly irritating. "You think I don't know that?" the American asked resentfully.

"You know now, I just told you," McKay said. Ringawa was bristling. "Saint George," McKay pointed out, "is the patron saint of Great Britain."

Ringawa glanced at Diego, who was poker-faced. "Well I say it's the Eve of Saint George," Ringawa said huffily, adjusting one of his earrings, "and let the fish and chips fall where they may."

Diego sighed. "Let's hope that garlic gets here on time," he said, changing the subject.

Ringawa brightened. "You said it," he drawled. "I love the smell of garlic in the morning."

9

Pulling a Fast One

"WHERE IS SEÑORA PERÓN?" asked Kegel, as he, Hitler, and the rest of Hitler's midnight dinner guests watched Oberschütze Spitz ladle the first glass of blood from the punch bowl.

"She informed the Führer she is not feeling well," Dorsch said, "and will not be dining this evening."

Hi, sitting by Dorsch, had expected Eva to use that excuse, which was why he didn't use it himself. He would have to try something else, and was nervous about it. He couldn't wait, though, to see these guys drinking this blood, which he knew came from one of the bottles he had spiked just an hour before. The other two bottles were being consumed at that moment in the Gebäude Zwei drink hall.

Hi looked at Müller and Frankel, seated across from him, as Spitz sat the first glass before Hitler at the head of the table. Hi figured his friends Müller and Frankel wouldn't be hungry, and no matter. He wondered if they felt anything yet.

"It's too bad about the señora," said Kegel, as Spitz served him his glass of blood. "The blood tonight looks—so rich."

Müller indeed wasn't hungry, and he felt nothing yet. But as he looked at Kegel, then Dorsch, he pitied the two pompous asses for not knowing the secret of the dragon's palm. Similarly, as Kegel looked at Müller, Kegel felt sorry for the ruthless nerd for not knowing the secret. Kegel felt no sympathy for Frankel for not knowing the secret, as Frankel was suspected of pilfering blood. Frankel, thinking he knew a secret they didn't know, felt superior to Kegel and Dorsch. Dorsch, who had been told the secret by Kegel so that Dorsch could decide how he knew, felt kind of sorry for Müller, but thought Frankel deserved to know zilch. What Kegel and Dorsch didn't know, but Müller did, was that Frankel knew better than to steal blood from Müller.

As for how Dorsch knew the palm's secret, he and Kegel agreed that Dorsch had been told by the Hauptsturmführer, who had happened to learn the secret, they decided, from Nova Dolencia's know-it-all shopkeeper, after mentioning the plant in his shop. It was then necessary for Kegel to tell the Hauptsturmführer the secret and how he knew it, in case Hitler asked him. Should the Hauptsturmführer tell the secret to anyone else, Kegel promised him a dip in the pool.

With everyone served, they were all free to drink, since there was never any blessing. Kegel, seated at Hitler's right hand, raised his glass first. Hi, looking past Dorsch, watched intently as Kegel put the glass to his lips and, to Hi's inner delight, drank almost a third of the glass with one backward tilt of his head.

"Ahhh," Kegel said, as he sat down the glass. "Plasmatic."

Hi watched as Dorsch beside him began drinking his glass of blood next. After the first big swallow, Dorsch gave a nod of approval to Müller. "Hemoglobinous," he said.

Hi felt almost victorious. He had Dorsch and Kegel, as he already had Müller and Frankel, who were only sipping their blood. But the big one remained. Hi was waiting for Hitler to drink. The Führer, ever since they first sat down, had been silent and pensive.

Hi watched now as Hitler picked up his glass of blood, and moved it slowly toward his mouth. Under the table Hi tapped himself quietly, rhythmically on the thigh with a fist, as if saying "Go, go" to Hitler. But the glass never reached Hitler's lips. To Hi's chagrin, Hitler sat it back down. Hitler seemed too preoccupied to drink.

"I have good news, my Schutzstaffel führers," Hitler said. It was the first words he had spoken that evening. "I have almost finished my memoirs."

The Nazis all exchanged glances, there were audible exhalations. "That *is* good news, mein Führer," Dorsch spoke for them all.

"We shall be laying plans," Hitler said calmly. "It is time to write a new chapter in the history of the thousand-year Reich."

Hitler's eyes fell upon Hi, then dropped to Hi's full glass of blood. Uh-oh, Hi thought, here it comes.

"Oberschütze Hickenlooper, you have not touched your blood. What is wrong?"

Hi cleared his throat. His excuse, he knew, was not going to sit well with Hitler or with Müller. He would just have to take the heat. In a few more hours, after all, there would hopefully be no heat to take.

"I'm afraid I'm not hungry, mein Führer," Hi said. "I had a snack, about an hour ago, at Obersturmbannführer Müller's." Hi saw Hitler start to frown; from the corner of his eye he saw Müller's jaw drop. "I was checking on the plants, and—"

"You had a *what* at Obersturmbannführer Müller's?" growled Hitler. There was stone silence at the table. Hitler's voice rose to a shout: "One does not snack at one's leisure on the blood supply of the Reich!"

Hitler's glaring eyes turned to Müller. The Obersturmbannführer was speechless. Hickenlooper was lying in a way, but then, in another way, he wasn't.

Hitler said ominously, "Obersturmbannführer Müller—"

"It was my fault, mein Führer," Hi jumped in. "I drank the blood before Oberstupidführer Müller—"

"Ober*sturm*bannführer," Müller corrected him. They were speaking in German, but in German the word "stupid" meant "stupid."

"I drank it before Herr Müller knew," Hi rephrased it. "It won't happen again. I can guarantee that. I'm sorry, mein Führer. Forgive me, Ober*sturm*bannführer."

For a moment there was silence. Hitler's anger could be seen to subside. He settled back in his chair, and gazed off into space for a moment. He began thinking about the order of business. Kegel and Dorsch, as Hi noted, resumed drinking their blood. But Hitler had yet to touch his.

"Obergruppenführer Dorsch..."

"Yes, mein Führer?"

Staring off, Hitler spoke measuredly, in pauses, thinking aloud. "I will soon send you to Peru.... What you will do... is spend an evening or two... giving General Belzu ... a complete overview... of what he may accrue... as reward for a coup."

Hi looked at Hitler with amazement. Unless Hi was mistaken, almost everything the Führer had just said would rhyme if spoken in English.

"A coup in Peru!" said Kegel, proposing a toast.

"Here's to!" said Dorsch.

All had raised their glasses, set to drink, except Hitler and Hi.

"Drink up, mein Führer," Kegel said politely. "You have not touched your blood either."

They waited for Hitler, deep in thought, to respond.

Finally he said, "This evening I shall fast."

Hi felt his heart sink.

"I always think best when I fast," Hitler said. He picked up his glassful of blood, and poured it back into the punch bowl.

Kegel was annoyed. His toast was still in suspension. He leaned forward to look at Hi, past Dorsch.

"Oberschütze," Kegel said, with that false smile of his, "will you not at least join us for a toast?" Kegel demonstratively lifted his glass, his eyes still on Hi. "To the coup in Peru."

Hi didn't know what to do. He saw all eyes, including Hitler's, upon him. He looked at his glass of blood. A glass of death. There was only one thing he *could* do. He picked up the glass, and poured the blood back into the bowl.

"I am fasting," Hi said, "with the Führer."

The Nazis were taken aback. Then Kegel said, "Not so fast. How can you fast? You have already snacked. You said so yourself."

"That is right," Dorsch said. "Simply not being hungry, that is not fasting."

"It certainly isn't," Frankel said.

"But I'm fasting right now," Hi explained.

"That is not a fair fast," Kegel said.

Frankel agreed, "It is not fair at all."

"We should have been told," Dorsch said. "We could all fast. But now we've partaken."

"Herr Hickenlooper, too, should partake," Frankel stated.

"He certainly should," Müller said.

"There is no way he can fast," Dorsch opined.

"He is pulling a fast one," said Kegel.

"That is right," Frankel said, "he—"

"Enough!" Hitler screamed.

Banging his fist on the table, Hitler rose to his feet. He was almost shaking with wrath, the officers cringing.

"Stop behaving like children! How am I to conquer the world," Hitler raged, his bulging eyes to the heavens, "if I am surrounded by such silly persons?" Jerking his head left and right as he shouted, Hitler pointed a shaking finger at Hi. "What difference does it make, you dim-witted twits, if this piddling planter is fasting?!"

"Why, none, mein Führer," Kegel said. "It makes no difference at all."

"Of course not," Müller said.

"Let him fast," Dorsch said with a wave of his hand.

"Who cares if he fasts or he doesn't?" Frankel asked.

Kegel was pleased to have the last word: "He is only a piddling planter."

Hi didn't mind being called piddling or anything else by these Aryan assholes. What he did mind was Hitler never touching that blood.

10

Bloody Sunrise

As DAWN WAS ABOUT TO BREAK, on the one hundred and twentieth day, Eva paced nervously in her quarters in her favorite black suit. With her was the Countess, who sat staring into space in her red satin gown. Countess Borca was thinking of her innocent Transylvanian childhood. It seemed like centuries ago, and it was. The two women waited, Eva worrying, trying to decide whether they should head for the jungle at first light, or wait for some possible word from Hi.

In his quarters Hitler, his tunic unbuttoned, sat at his desk, listening to Wagner music on a hi-fi powered by a generator running in a room below. Fitted on Hitler's hands were two hand puppets—Stalin and Hitler—pummeling each other while Hitler refereed.

In the jungle thicket McKay, Diego, Ringawa, and their eager mercenaries tensely waited for the first signs of light, and the first sound of aircraft approaching.

At the picnic table in front of Gebäude Ein, Kegel and Dorsch sat playing a game of cards. Other Nazis moved about on the grounds, some heading for Gebäude Zwei to get ready for another day's sleep.

Near the table Hi idly paced. He had spent most of the night with the Führer after dinner, discussing those damnable memoirs. Hitler wouldn't yield on even the most ridiculous points, such as his contention that the British had secretly *asked* Nazi Germany to bomb them, to help test their air defenses. Now, as dawn neared, Hi had ostensibly been watching the Obergruppenführers' card game, but his eyes kept moving eastward, looking for those first rays of light, then westward, for some garlic from Canutama, then eastward again, where some buddies from Nova Dolencia, he hoped, were lurking in the foliage. Hi was worrying, too, about Eva and the Countess. They had to be out of Neuanfang before the garlic arrived. And it damn sure better arrive, Hi thought, because so far the dragon's blood was having no visible effect at all.

Kegel was in a good mood—and not because he was winning the card game, which he always did. He had a date later on with the Countess. He had been to see Müller about his blood type. Müller told him that it didn't matter, that vampires could suck any type. Kegel said that nonetheless he had to know what his was. Müller, who didn't want to be bothered—he was waiting for the effect of DPE to kick in—told Kegel that the answer was simple. All members of the master race, Müller said, were Type A Plus. Kegel marveled, saying, "You learn something new every day."

Dorsch was mad, and not because of the card game. He had been mad ever since dinner. "Dim-witted twits. That's what he called us," Dorsch grumbled, studying another bad hand. "Did you hear, Kegel? We are dim-witted twits."

As he was listening, Hi saw it: the first glow of sunrise behind the black wall of jungle.

"Don't take it so personally, Dorsch," Kegel said. "You will soon be going to Lima. Be glad."

"Bah! To travel means having to scavenge, not knowing where your next meal is coming from."

"Then may I go in your stead?"

" 'Dim-witted twits,' " Dorsch mumbled.

Kegel suddenly noticed with amazement that Dorsch, unawares, had smoke coming out of his ears.

"Obergruppenführer, you are fuming," Kegel said.

"Of course I am fuming. Shouldn't you be?"

Hi, his eyes on the dawning light, suddenly turned, realizing what he had heard. He saw Dorsch smoking, beginning to gasp, and Hi couldn't help smiling.

Hi heard a man scream, turned, and saw the Hauptsturmführer come stumbling out of Gebäude Drei. The Nazi was bleeding from mouth, nose, and ears. He was shaking, smoking, and screaming. Then, as the Hauptsturmführer fell to his knees, other screams of agony on the compound began.

Kegel, dumbfounded, rose from the table. He, too, was beginning to smoke. "Mein Führer!" he yelled, in sudden searing pain. All over the compound SS men, some just having landed from the night's bat patrol, were bleeding, screaming, and falling. Hi had the impression that the first light of day helped hasten the extract's effect.

As Kegel rushed unsteadily for Gebäude Ein, Hi watched Dorsch begin to bloat where he sat, his immobilized body slowly bursting open, blood pouring from his massively rupturing flesh.

Hi turned and ran for Gebäude Zwei and his gas mask. The planes, if they came, wouldn't know if they were needed or not. According to plan, they would dust first and ask questions later.

Hitler, oblivious to the screaming outside as Wagner music filled the chamber, was still refereeing his puppet fight when Kegel came bursting—literally—in. Hitler rose to his feet at the horrid sight, as swollen Kegel, bleeding and choking, staggered to the desk. Hitler, with no time to get rid of the puppets, hoped Kegel wouldn't notice them.

"Mein Führer," Kegel croaked like a frog, bloating, expanding—then suddenly exploding, in a red blur of blood and flesh.

Hitler looked around in amazement. Just as Hickenlooper had dreamt, Kegel had filled his quarters with a thousand bloody pieces of himself. There were even bits all over Hitler.

"Kegel!" shouted the Führer, "is this some kind of joke?"

Hi, gas mask in hand, rushed into Eva's quarters. He hustled Eva and the Countess to the door. "Get out of here fast. Head for the jungle. Go east, away from the compound."

The Countess headed out, but Eva said, "Hi, let me stay. There must be some way I can help."

"You can help by getting away, so I'll know that you're safe." Hi grabbed her by the arm. "God knows what'll happen when that garlic gets here. Now let's go."

That garlic had McKay in a bind. It was dawn. He and his men could hear screaming from the compound, and a commando was dispatched through the several yards of thick jungle between their position and the clearing for a look. But the garlic wasn't there yet.

"What do you think?" Diego asked. "We better go in."

"You're damn right," said Ringawa. More screams from the compound.

"It could be a Nazi trick," one commando warned.

"Yeah, these are vampires, man," said another.

"Where's that damn garlic?" said a third.

McKay had to decide. He looked at his watch. "We'll give it two minutes to get here."

"We gotta go in!" Ringawa yelled at him.

"Disobey me," McKay warned Ringawa, "and I'll have your golden locks shorn."

The commando dispatched to the clearing peeked out

wide-eyed from the thicket. Several Nazis, dead or dying, lay around on the compound in big pools of blood. The commando saw a striking woman in red hurrying in his general direction, while behind her another woman, who appeared to be Eva Perón, stopped and looked back.

Meanwhile Hi rushed into the Weinberg. He found Frankel and Spitz in their death throes, bloating, swaying on their feet, Spitz clinging to his superior in their confusion and agony.

Hi grabbed the two chummily by the shoulders. "How's it going, mush heads?" he asked, and clobbered their heads together. They burst open like two blood-filled melons.

Crowley lay all but dead on his bunk. He struggled weakly to his feet as he heard the rattle of a key unlocking cell doors. "Everybody out and head for the jungle!" he heard Hi saying. "Head east and wait! Get off of the compound!"

Hi appeared outside Crowley's cell. "I see you made it, pal," Hi smiled, unlocking the door. "Way to go."

Meanwhile Hitler had discovered the split-open body of Bingle near the door of his quarters. Poor Bingle had apparently tried his best to get to work that morning. With a Luger pistol in hand, an SS dagger on his hip, Hitler descended the stairs. Heading for the Gebäude Ein main hall, he saw the Scharführer, bleeding and bloating, coming toward him. Hitler stopped as the Scharführer, much more confused than usual, staggered up to him.

"Mein—" That's as far as the Scharführer got. Blood spewed from his mouth, and before Hitler's eyes he began deflating like a baloon. "Fuuuuuuuuuuuuu...."

Outside, with morning light on the compound, Hitler headed straight for Gebäude Drei. He walked past SS bodies lying in their blood, with dying SS men calling out to him pleadingly. The Führer ignored them. Of what use were the dead and the dying?

Hitler was going to Munitions. From there he would defend Neuanfang, from whatever was happening, if he had to do it all by himself.

11

Die Happy

THE ROTTENFÜHRER stepped out of Munitions. He had been sick all night from some jungle bug. Skipping dinner, he had tried to work on his monthly inventory—he was getting low on firecrackers and marbles, and was still missing a gas mask—but had fallen asleep. Feeling somewhat better, he yawned—then was startled to see Hitler, a Luger in hand, enter the corridor and approach him.

"Heil Hitler," the Rottenführer said, snapping to attention with a click of his heels.

"Forget that shit," Hitler said. "Everything in Munitions okay?"

"Yes, mein Führer. What is wrong?"

Hitler looked at him curiously. "There is nothing wrong with you?"

"I've got a bad stomach, mein Führer. I couldn't drink a drop of blood last night."

"You didn't drink any blood?" Hitler thought for a moment. "Nor did Hickenlooper."

"What is wrong, sir?"

"Wrong? We are under attack, you Schwachsinnige!" With the Rottenführer available here, Hitler decided to take another look outside. "Guard Munitions," Hitler ordered, and headed down the corridor.

Outside, Hi, his gas mask secured to his belt, paused to watch Crowley and the other freed captives fleeing toward the jungle, the stronger ones helping the weaker. SS men were too busy dying to stop them. Hi turned and looked toward the balcony of Hitler's quarters. Where was the Führer? About to head for Gebäude Ein, Hi saw, from the corner of his eye, someone step out of Gebäude Drei. Hi turned to look.

It was Hitler.

So this is the enemy, Hitler thought. He had let himself be bamboozled. Hi and Hitler began approaching each other slowly, eyes locked. Hitler still held the Luger, useless, of course, against a vampire. Within a few feet of each other they stopped. They stood in virtually the center of Neuanfang, the dead and the dying scattered around them. One dying Schütze, then another, called out in a gurgle, "Mein Führer..."

Hi and Hitler stared at each other with calm mutual hatred.

Hitler discarded the Luger. "Oberschütze," he rasped. He unsheathed his SS dagger.

"Mein Führer," Hi said, drawing his dagger too.

"You are behind this. You are one of my mistakes, Oberschütze."

"What do you plan to do about it?"

"First, I demote you. You are nothing but a Schütze again."

Hi smiled. "Who is left, besides you, to outrank me?"

They heard someone come out of Gebäude Drei. They both glanced over to see who it was.

The Rottenführer, looking around in shock at the inexplicable carnage on the compound, drew his dagger and walked toward Hi. Flanking Hitler, he stopped a few feet from the American.

Hi had quit smiling. But he was standing his ground. "Okay," he said to Hitler with a nod toward the

Rottenführer, "who else besides him?"

Hitler glanced at the Rottenführer. "I ordered you to stay at Munitions." He said it good-naturedly.

"But I desire to assist you, mein Führer." The Rottenführer was staring coldly at Hi.

"Well, then," Hitler said. With a smile he told Hi, "You are a dead little Schütze."

Hitler and the Rottenführer stepped warily toward Hi with their daggers. Hi took a fighting stance with his. But the Nazis then stopped. All three of them heard something, faint, but getting louder, as they looked off toward the west. About damn time, Hi thought. It was the Canutama planes.

The Dusty Dragon, Eat My Dust, and Duster Offer were flying in formation, fairly low over the jungle, for their first pass over Neuanfang, already in the three pilots' sight. The pilots had had to estimate the distance and flight time, and could only hope, assuming that the powder was needed, that it wasn't too late.

Hitler, thinking they were fighter planes as he saw them approach in the distance, looked at Hi with amusement. "Ha! They think to destroy me with bullets or bombs?" Hitler knew he was protected by vampire physics, though Einstein himself would have trouble explaining it. Like so-called virtual particles, coming and going in the quantum vacuum, a vampire's body, if destroyed, would with few exceptions—such as destruction by a stake or a Schutzstaffel dagger—immediately reassemble itself. And remain undead. Thus vampires, as in some sense vacuum fluctuations, made quantum theory a darker side of the cosmos.

Of course, the effect on vampires of a thick cloud of garlic powder remained to be seen. Unwittingly Hitler was to be a test case. Turning toward the oncoming planes,

Hitler lifted his arms, dagger raised, offering himself in defiant disdain.

"Here I am!" Hitler screamed at the planes, on course to fly straight over his head. "Let me have it!"

As soon as the planes reached the clearing, and began releasing their garlic powder, Hitler saw that these were not fighters. And he knew he must be in trouble when he saw the descending, roiling, dustlike cloud, and with a glance at Hi saw him putting on a gas mask.

Hitler barely had time to lower his arms before the thick swirl of garlic powder enveloped him, the Rottenführer, and Hi. Hitler, wheezing, lungs seared, eyes burning, fell to his knees. The Rottenführer reeled, desperately trying to breathe. Hi, masked and unaffected, couldn't see either Nazi in the blanketing cloud, but heard Hitler gaspingly order, "Kill him! Killll him!" Hi moved in Hitler's direction, dagger set to strike, but then saw the staggering Rottenführer, dagger raised, come at him out of the blinding swirl.

Hi stabbed the crazed Rottenführer in the chest, barely missing the heart, as the Nazi, his dagger slicing Hi's shoulder, collided with him. They both fell to the ground, while Hitler struggled to his feet in the thinning garlic cloud. While Hi and the Rottenführer, both still with daggers in hand, wrestled on the ground, Hitler hurried toward Gebäude Drei. Half-maddened by the garlic, the Führer did a crazy-jointed dance as he went.

The Rottenführer was too crazed by the garlic to put up a good fight. Rolling up on top of him, Hi plunged his dagger deep into the Nazi's heart. Dropping his dagger, the mortally wounded Rottenführer thought he was seeing some beatific vision as he looked up into Hi's masked face.

"Mein Führer!" the dying Nazi called out. "Mein Führer, I found it! The missing gas mask!"

The Rottenführer died happy.

As Hi ran after the Führer, the crop dusters were banking, to come back for their second pass. McKay, Diego, and the commandos had donned their gas masks, and were crashing through the thicket for the clearing, at the edge of which, according to plan, they would wait for the instant of the second powder release before charging the compound, to tangle with any surviving undead.

When the Countess and released captives had come upon the team, McKay told them to keep heading east, as far away as they could get, and then wait. None of them were going to argue. Even at this distance the Countess was about to die from the garlic, holding a handkerchief tight over her nose, as she simultaneously half-carried the weak Crowley eastward through the jungle.

"What in heaven's name are they using?" Crowley asked, coughing from powder drifting eastward in the air.

The Countess, understanding no English, thought she heard "Eva" in his question. "She is probably dead," she said in Romanian as she pulled Crowley onward. "The foolish woman went back to help."

12

A Blast in Gebäude Drei

FRENZIED EVA grabbed a gas mask and put it on. She had stayed behind in Neuanfang with a last-minute notion of running to Adolf, to be with him in his hour of need, thereby being at his side to help destroy him somehow when the Newfangled operatives struck. Her relationship with Hitler had been estranged since long before Hi's arrival, Hitler being aware of her disillusionment and depression, and the possibility had even existed, she knew, that the Führer would simply do away with her, as he had got rid of Eva Braun. Surely, Eva thought, Adolf would welcome her back upon seeing her feigned recommitment to him in this desperate hour. But she had been unable to find him before the garlic raid, which caught her as she came out the front entrance of Gebäude Ein, where she had searched for him. Fearful of dying, she had run through the blinding cloud in what she hoped was the direction of Gebäude Drei. Right on target, she ran into the side of the building, almost knocking herself out. She barely made it inside to Munitions and a gas mask before she would have passed out from the garlic.

As she was recovering, gulping air in the mask in Munitions, she heard jackboots approach on the run in the corridor. Her only thought was to hide, her half-baked notion of trying to cozy up to Hitler abandoned. All she wanted to do now was find Hi. Getting quickly to the floor, she began crawling quietly down an aisle between stacks of assorted equipment, as she heard the jackboots run into the room. Rounding a corner in the aisle, Eva raised herself high enough to peek over the equipment, and saw that it was Hitler himself gulping air from a gas mask.

Strapping the mask onto his head, Hitler rushed to a collection of submachine guns, on a table on the far side of the room. He did not yet know what kind of force in addition to Hickenlooper he was dealing with. But Hitler knew of no beings except vampires who could take submachine-gun bullets with impunity.

No sooner did Hitler grab up a loaded submachine gun than Hi, still wearing his mask, his dagger dripping Rottenführer blood, came rushing into the room. Hi stopped, looked around, and didn't see Hitler, who had gone into a crouch. Then the Führer stood suddenly erect. Hitler didn't even know it was Hi as he sprayed him with bullets, sending Hi careening backward against a stack of equipment and then to the floor.

For a moment Hi, covered with bloody wounds, was out if not dead. Eva, hiding by some frogman equipment, feared the worst. But in the next moment Hi was getting back to his feet, shaken but hardly worse for the wear. "Mein Führer," Hi called to him mockingly, "you think to destroy me with bullets or bombs?"

Hitler had picked up a hand grenade. Seeing it was Hi who opposed him, Hitler pulled the pin anyway. "I'll try anything once, Schütze!" he called back, and threw the grenade at him.

Hi instinctively ducked down into an aisle. The grenade hit the wall, bounced over into Eva's aisle, and exploded. Hi watched in amazement as Eva, holding something in her hand, was blown into the air, to land in a neighboring aisle, amid a rain of debris.

A BLAST IN GEBÄUDE DREI

Hitler, looking for Hi, advanced along the tables of equipment with the submachine gun. Picking up the gun again during the explosion, and still wearing his sight-limiting gas mask, Hitler had failed to see flying Eva. Enough bullets, Hitler thought, ought to wear Hickenlooper down. They would at least keep him off his feet for a while.

Bleeding Hi, on his hands and knees, frantically yanked off his gas mask. He couldn't find his dagger, which he had dropped when hit by the bullets. Then he saw Eva crawl out from an adjoining aisle. Dazed, she looked awful, hair frizzled, suit tattered, her gas mask hanging in shreds from her blackened face. She slid something across the floor to Hi. She had held onto it right through the explosion. Grabbing it up, Hi saw that it was a frogman's spring-powered spear gun, its barbed spear ready to fire. Thank God and Eva, Hi thought, it hadn't discharged in the blast.

Hi fleetingly saw Hitler's masked head moving behind an equipment stack as the Führer approached the corner of Hi's aisle. From the floor Hi aimed the spear gun at the corner, just high enough to shoot for the Führer's heart. Hitler came past the corner, turned to aim the submachine gun, and Hi fired the spear gun.

Hitler screamed as the spear pierced his body. Going straight through his heart, the spear's barbed, bloodied head stuck out of his back. Dropping the gun, Hitler kept from falling by propping a hand on the corner table. His other hand took hold of the shaft, but the spear was too firmly embedded, and Hitler too suddenly weakened, for him to pull it out of the blood-pouring wound.

Hitler glared through his mask at Hi, who stared back, hoping to watch Hitler die. But Hitler disappointed him. After a moment the Führer reached down, picked up the submachine gun with effort, and staggered toward the door.

Hi went quickly to Eva, who sat up and leaned against a table leg as Hi knelt beside her. She was still dazed from the blast.

"I thought I told you to get off the compound," he said softly, putting a hand to her face.

"Why the hell didn't I listen?" she said.

"Get another mask and get going," Hi said. "I'm going after Hitler." He looked around and saw his dagger under a table. Retrieving it and his mask, he smiled back at Eva, said "Thanks for that spear gun," and headed for the door.

13

"What an Ouch!"

THE CROP DUSTERS had just made their second pass as Hi hurried out of Gebäude Drei. He saw Hitler, bent with pain, hurrying toward Gebäude Vier before the new cloud of garlic powder enveloped him.

Hi went after him as swiftly as he dared, moving blindly through the swirling cloud. At the same time, McKay, Diego, Ringawa, and their commandos charged from the east wall of jungle, fanning out cautiously over the dust-shrouded compound, and stopping to drive stakes into any Nazis still breathing.

Hitler entered the Water Control Room. Leaving the door open and discarding his gas mask, he leaned for a moment on a console, to muster what strength had not yet been sapped by the spear still stuck through his heart. He felt he was dying, but he planned at least to take with him the traitorous Hickenlooper, who at that moment was surely coming after him.

Dropping his submachine gun, Hitler staggered to the Large Important Lever and pulled it down, grimacing with pain at the effort. He heard the grinding sound of the underwater tunnel opening, which would release piranhas into the conversion pool. He then went to the door leading to the pool platform, opened it, turned, and leaned against the door jamb, conserving the last of his strength. He was waiting for Hi to arrive.

Meanwhile McKay and Ringawa, still wearing gas masks, their submachine guns at ready, burst into Hitler's quarters. Wagner still played on the hi-fi. They made a quick search, stepping in and around the blood and grisly pieces of Kegel's remains.

Ringawa looked revulsed. "My God," he said, "what kind of music is that?"

"Wagner," McKay said, turning. "Let's go."

McKay headed out, but there was something Ringawa had to do. Aiming his submachine gun, he riddled the hi-fi with bullets.

Searching for Hitler in Gebäude Vier, Hi, with dagger in hand, cautiously approached the open door to the Water Control Room. Hi had never been anywhere in Vier except Müller's blood ministry. Looking in the door, Hi saw Hitler across the room, standing in a doorway, looking back at him. Beyond the doorway Hi saw only darkness, from which came, he thought, the faint sound of a generator. Hitler's submachine gun lay on the control room floor. Hitler turned and went out the doorway, closing the door behind him.

Entering the control room, Hi glanced curiously around at its gadgets, then hurried across to the door where Hitler had exited. Holding his dagger at ready, Hi opened the door. He looked into the darkness, then cautiously moved through the door. From behind the door Hitler shoved and simultaneously tripped him, sending Hi tumbling forward on the platform, which measured only ten feet to the edge. With all his strength Hitler then shoved Hi with a foot. Rolling off the edge of the platform, Hi managed to grab the edge with one hand, then the other, and was left hanging by his hands over the pool. Glancing down at the water, lit under the surface, he saw piranhas swimming in a circle, as if eagerly awaiting him.

Hi looked up at Hitler, who stepped to the platform's edge and looked gloatingly down at Hi.

"Mein Führer," Hi said, desperately holding on to the edge, Hitler's jackboots but inches from Hi's fingers, "you expect to destroy me with piranhas?"

"You bet," Hitler smiled, as he positioned a foot over one of Hi's hands. "Ever seen those things bite?"

Eva, wearing a new gas mask, was hurrying toward Gebäude Vier when the crop dusters made their third pass. She had guessed that was where Hitler headed after leaving Munitions. Gebäude Ein with its telltale balcony and swastika would be swarmed by commandos, and in Gebäude Zwei there would be mostly dead Schützes. In Vier was the last of the blood supply, at least a bottle of which Hitler might try to take with him before trying to flee the compound—if he had not already done so or been caught by commandos.

Hurrying toward Gebäude Vier, Eva spotted some commandos checking SS bodies, and called to them. But the gas mask muffled her voice, and as the third cloud of garlic powder descended, she lost sight of the commandos and of Gebäude Vier too. She continued hurrying in Vier's general direction. She ran into the side of the building, almost knocking herself out. What did I do, she thought, to deserve such a beating?

Going into Vier, the first door Eva came to was that of the Water Control Room. She cautiously entered it.

Barely a moment later, Diego and two commandos, with gas masks and submachine guns, entered the building from the opposite side. They burst into the Weinberg. While the two commandos searched there, Diego proceeded to the Weinkellar door. He kicked it in and entered. He was immediately grabbed around the neck from behind by Müller, who was bleeding and bloating.

The DPE had finally kicked in, so to speak.

Vainly struggling, Diego was about to lose consciousness, overpowered by the vampire's chokehold. With his free hand Müller raised his SS dagger. But before he could plunge the dagger into Diego's neck, the dragon's blood *really* kicked in. Müller emitted a horrific scream, and exploded, Diego dropping to the floor from the grasp of suddenly nothing.

Hitler, continuing to lose strength, was stepping on and kicking at Hi's hands, Hi desperately moving his hands this way and that as he clung to the platform's edge.

"Adolf!" they suddenly heard Eva say. Turning unsteadily, Hitler looked at Eva, who had stepped out of the control room.

Taking off her gas mask, Eva didn't know where she was, and had no idea that Hi, in the darkness behind Hitler, was hanging from the platform. She knew only that she was going to cozy up to Hitler, hold him there till Hi or some commandos arrived.

"There you are!" Eva said, feigning relief. "Adolf, what has happened? Everyone's dying."

"You are all right?" Hitler asked. He was amazed that she was, then remembered she had skipped last night's meal. As Hitler spoke, behind him Eva saw Hi lift himself up enough to peek over the platform's edge.

Eva was visibly surprised, but then masked it by feigning horror at the sight of Hitler's spear wound. "Adolf, what an ouch!" she said. Dropping the gas mask, she stepped toward Hitler, as Hi got an elbow onto the platform. "You will die with that thing in your chest. Won't it come out?" She gently took hold of the shaft sticking out of his chest. "Let me help."

Grabbing one of Hitler's ankles, Hi hollered, "Now!"

Eva shoved on the spear, Hi shoved the opposite way

"WHAT AN OUCH!"

on the ankle, and Hitler, falling backwards right over Hi, went headlong into the water.

Hi looked up at Eva. Off-balance from shoving Hitler, she was teetering on the edge of the platform, waving her arms, trying to keep from falling into the water, where the piranhas had started a feeding frenzy on Hitler.

Hi, clinging to the edge, couldn't reach her, he was helpless, as Eva swayed, her arms flailing the air.

"Eva," Hi said softly, "don't—"

Eva fell screaming into the water.

"Eva!" Hi cried, and let go of the edge, falling in right behind her.

14

"The Easy Part's Over"

SURFACING RIGHT OVER the feeding piranhas, Hi and Eva began swimming desperately toward the side of the pool. Diego, with submachine gun in hand, emerged from the control room and looked down into the pool. Seeing piranhas, just under the water's surface, swimming after Hi and Eva, Diego immediately began firing his gun, raking the water behind the fleeing pair with bullets, scaring off any fish that weren't killed, till Hi and Eva, suffering a few painful nips, reached the side of the pool and pulled themselves out of the water.

McKay and Ringawa, followed by several commandos, arrived on the platform, and looked down with Diego at the piranhas' feast. From the bottom of the pool dead eyes stared up from what was left of Hitler's face under the billowing blood. The spear in his chest was falling slowly to one side, little flesh left to hold it up, as the piranhas continued their underwater frenzy.

"End of Hitler Part Two," said Diego.

"All the other Nazis are dead," McKay reported.

"I got to stake two of 'em personally," Ringawa said proudly, "before they could die on me."

McKay looked over at Hi. He and Eva sat catching their breath near the side of the pool. "He did one hell of a job," said the man from IQ.

"You okay?" Hi asked Eva.

Eva nodded yes. "Except for the shrapnel," she said, referring to grenade fragments in her body. "It's a pain."

"I know what you mean," Hi said, rubbing his blood-soaked midriff. "I'd like to get these bullets out."

They looked at each other. "Well, the easy part's over," Hi said. "Now comes the hard part."

"What's that?"

"I've got to lose you again. The president wants his wife back."

Eva smiled. "He can't have her," she said. "She's dead." Hi, gazing at her, wondered if she really meant it. Eva leaned over and gave him a kiss. "He's already told the *world* she's dead."

"So Juan has to lose her again?" Hi asked.

"That's right. I'll send him a 'Dear Juan' letter. Personal and confidential."

Hi felt sorry for that wimp in BA. Hi knew exactly how it felt to lose her. But he felt pretty good for himself. Hi smiled and said, "Let get back for that cure."

She was worried. "Hi, what if the cure doesn't work?"

"Don't even think that. It's got to."

Edgar Hickenlooper was determined to see that it did. A week after Operation Newfangled's success, Hi and Eva were at the Florida mansion, where Edgar intended to keep them till cured. Hi, Eva, and Diego had left the compound immediately, escorting the Countess and freed captives to Nova Dolencia, leaving McKay and the others to see to the compound's demolition. No trace was to remain of Neuanfang's existence.

Edgar flew Dr. Po up from BA to supervise the cure, with an upstairs room of the mansion specially redesigned for the purpose. On the fifth day of the ordeal, Edgar, Po, and Diego stood outside the room at a one-way observation window and watched the couple's progress.

"The secret, of course," Po smiled, "was my discovery that even vampire bats—born vampires—can be weaned off blood and learn to eat other creatures."

Edgar shook his head, still amazed by it all. "Who would have thought," he said, "with all the legends and myths about vampires, that you could lick it by going cold turkey?"

Inside the padded cell, Hi and Eva, both breathing heavily, took a break from thrashing around, though still restrained in their straitjackets.

"How you doing?" Hi gasped.

"I couldn't make it without you," Eva said, gasping too.

"Same here." After they rested a few moments, Hi tried to kiss her, but their awkward positions made it impossible. They began moving around, trying to get into position for a smooch.

"God, I hope this cure works," Eva said.

"It will," Hi said confidently, moving, almost in position to kiss her. "Oh, we'll always be wanting some blood. We'll just have to be strong."

He was finally in position, his face over hers. They gazed into each other's eyes. "Anyway, it was worth it," Hi said softly. "We got Hitler. Together. We got him. What do you say to that, my first lady?"

Eva smiled. Just before their lips met, she whispered, "Heil Hickenlooper."